Barbara Dugan

GOOD-BYE, HELLO

Greenwillow Books, New York

Library of Congress Cataloging-in-Publication Data
Dugan, Barbara.
     Good-bye, hello / by Barbara Dugan.
          p.   cm.
     Summary: While she is in the sixth grade, twelve-year-old Bobbie's two problems are adjusting to class with Sister Alice and realizing that her grandmother is old and in poor health.
     ISBN 0-688-12447-X
     [1. Teachers—Fiction.
2. Catholic schools—Fiction.
3. Schools—Fiction.
4. Grandmothers—Fiction.]   I. Title.
PZ7.D87817Go   1994
[Fic]—dc20
93-10989   CIP   AC

For the sisters of
St. Bartholomew School, 1962–1970,
and
in memory of my grandmother

CHAPTER 1

"Knee to chest!" Dad hollers from the back of the boat.

I dig the edge of my ski into the sand and adjust the foothold. The rubber flaps slide together, covering my foot like two big lips. My knee *is* tucked to my chest.

The day is turning to evening, but the air is still warm. Even half in and half out of the water with my orange life jacket dripping, I'm not that cold. The skiing conditions are perfect. The bay is so calm the water looks as if it had been ironed flat.

"Punch it, Dad."

"You're not ready. I can see you're not ready. Get in position."

"I *am* in position, Dad. You just can't see me."

"I can see you fine, Bobbie."

A boat roars by pulling a skier. *Splat!* The skier just jumped the entire width of the wake. In the calm part of the water now, he leans to the side and sprays us.

Beads of water smack me. Beachball-size waves bounce me around.

"Wah-hoo!" The boys in the speeding boat look back and wave.

"I've got your number!" Dad shouts after them.

This is my first time slaloming. But I've been skiing on two skis since I was six, and I figure that makes me a pro and ready for one.

Dad doesn't think so. He thinks two skis are fine. He says I get my daring ways from Gramma Callahan. He claims Sylvester, his older brother, stole his share of daringness and left him with nothing but Grandpa's pure caution.

We're close to the shore, so I can start off in shallow water. Gramma is behind me on the dock of our boat slip, resting in her portable lounger, wearing her thongs, and cheering me on. Everything is perfect, and will be until tomorrow.

"Left leg back," Dad yells. "Don't be in a rush. Let the boat pull you up."

"This is Sea World, Dad. I'm skiing with twelve other people. They're waiting. My partner is waiting, too, on top of my shoulders. She's heavy. Hit it!"

"I mean it, Bobbie. I'm serious. There are a lot of other boats in this bay. You pay attention to what you're doing."

"I will, Dad."

"Your mother counts five. *Five* other skiers in this bay, going in all different directions."

Mom stands and points out the other boats.

2

My sister, Elissa, copies her.

My bathing suit has pink sequins sewn to it. My head-band has a feather. I'm wearing waterproof green glitter eye shadow. Lots of it. The killer whale act is tough to follow, but I can do it. My fans are expecting big things from me.

"Steady yourself before you slip that back leg in the ski, Bobbie," Dad says. "And if you stay up—"

"If!"

"—stay in the wake and get your bearings before you attempt to cross over," Dad finishes. He takes a swig from his tumbler and sinks down into the driver's seat. He adjusts the rearview mirror.

I grip the plastic rope bar.

Dad trolls, and the motor makes puttering sounds.

The ski rope straightens and tightens, tugging at my arms and pulling me forward through the water.

"Hit it!" I yell.

The motor roars.

Water explodes around me. It rushes over my shoulders and flies up into my face. And then it's just the air. I'm out of the water. I did it! I'm up!

I'm down.

"I could have stayed up if you had just waited, Dad."

"Eleven tries is plenty, Bobbie," Dad says. "You can't be in such a hurry to put that back foot in the ski."

We're driving down County Road 15, which winds

3

around the shore of the lake. I'm sitting on a soggy towel in the backseat. My hair is hanging in wet clumps. "I almost had it, Dad."

"I know you did, sweetie. Next summer you'll get it for sure."

"That's a year away, Dad. A whole year."

The windows are down. Dad's sunburned arm is resting over the door. The wind is blowing his hair back, what little he has of it.

Mom is fidgeting with the radio dial, trying to find a news station. Mom is a nut for news.

It's eight-twenty according to the car clock, which is five minutes fast, which, when you're counting minutes, is important.

Elissa isn't in the car with us. She's with Gram, looking stupid in that motorcycle helmet Dad makes her wear every time she rides in Gramma's convertible.

It's a 1967 Pontiac convertible: sky blue, all leather interior, bucket seats, automatic windows, tape deck, no rust. Dad says it makes Gram feel independent to drive her own car. But I know she drives for the fun of it. In all kinds of summer weather except for rain Gramma cruises with the top down. She wears a silk scarf tied to her head and squeezes every mile she can out of the car before it sits in our garage all winter like a showroom model.

County Road 15 is curvy. Our car eases around the bends. Our headlights point at people fishing from the shore. They're holding their rods in one hand and slap-

4

ping mosquitoes off themselves with the other hand. In the water, boats are moving with their lights on, making shiny trails wherever they go.

"Please don't kick my seat, Bobbie," Dad says.

I tuck my legs under me. News talk is coming out of the back speakers. "Dad, I might not be able to slalom next summer. I might not make it through this school year."

Mom bends her head down.

"Go ahead, laugh, Mom."

"I'm sorry, Bobbie, but you're so dramatic."

"I hate it when you laugh at me."

Mom turns and faces me. "I'm sorry," she says. "We know this school year is going to be different without Charlotte."

My stomach feels empty as I think about school. I've tried not to think about it much over the summer.

Charlotte Joan Hansen. Bobbie Jean Callahan. Before she left in June, we gave each other friendship rings and vowed to be best friends forever.

This summer it didn't seem as if Charlotte was really gone. Not for good. It just seemed like every other summer when her family packed up and took off for Cape Cod. I keep hoping that it's all a joke about their moving away, and tomorrow, when I go to school, Charlotte will be there.

I'll sneak up behind her and clap my hands over her eyes. "Guess who?"

Charlotte will scream. Charlotte loves to scream. Then

she'll peel my hands off her face, and we'll both scream: *"You're home!"*

Next Charlotte will stoop down with her backpack and pull out a package.

A present? For me, Charlotte? I'll act surprised, but I know it's a charm. Every summer she picks me out a new one. I have a charm in the shape of Connecticut and one in the shape of Delaware. I have a pelican from Maine with a mouth that really opens and a fish inside.

Until the second bell rings, Charlotte will tell me all about the ocean, and the states she crossed, and how many times she got sick in the car. I'll tell her about the cabin, and my birthday party in June that she misses every year, and Summer Playhouse, and the lake, and all the places I've been to on my bike. At recess I'll show her my new routines. I'll do a couple of commercials for her.

But it's no use thinking this way. Why hope? Tomorrow Charlotte won't be in school. At least she won't be at Saint Francis. She'll be starting a public school in Pittsburgh. There won't be anyone at school waiting especially for me.

Suddenly Mom hushes Dad. He was humming. Her ear is down by the radio. Someplace, far away, a war is starting.

I hold my arm out the window.

"Do you want a truck to come along and cut off that arm?" Dad asks.

"Sh-h," Mom says.

6

The moon is hanging down over the water like a giant white cookie.

A press conference by the President is being aired. Reporters are shout talking, trying to get their questions answered. "Mr. President," they're saying. "Mr. President . . ."

Have you noticed that radio announcers always have voices like no one else? I plug my nose and lower my voice: "G-o-o-d evening."

"Bobbie!" Mom snaps.

For three Christmases in a row now I've asked for a microphone, but I've never gotten one.

Behind our car, as usual, there are a ton of other cars. No one in the world drives as slowly as my dad. I close my eyes. I'm thinking about root beer. Every year on this same night we drive to Wagners in Hopkins for root beer. It's a tradition. Drinking root beer is the way our family says good-bye to the summer. Sure, a couple of places around here serve root beer, but they don't bring it out to your car in cold glass mugs. At Wagners you get to order from your own speakerphone. The people that work there wear change machines around their waists, and they don't ask if you want french fries or cherry pies, if you didn't say so in the first place.

"Enough bad news," Mom says. She shuts the radio off and turns to me. Her face is shadowy in the dark of the car. "It's usually worse thinking about something than actually doing it, Bobbie. At least that's what I've found. It will be tough without Charlotte at school, but

7

I still think you're going to have a good year. Sister Alice is an excellent teacher."

"She'll shape you kids up," Dad says.

"We don't need shaping up, Dad."

"Bobbie," Mom says, "you've had all fairly lenient teachers at Saint Francis up until this point. Your father and I both feel that a shot of the old school ways is exactly what you need."

"I think I need to be home schooled."

"Home schooled!" Mom shrieks.

"What?" Dad says. "Do you want us to quit our jobs?"

"Gramma could do it," I tell them.

"My poor mother," he says.

"Seriously, Bobbie," Mom says, "your grandmother has her own life. I think we ask her to do enough as it is."

"I could take a year off, then," I tell them. "Do an independent study. I read a book about a boy who took a year off and lived in a tree. I could do that and write a report. Teachers love reports."

"Yah, right," Dad says.

Eight forty-two P.M. Six hundred eighty-eight minutes to go. Six hundred eighty-eight minutes left of freedom. Then the first bell rings, and it's nothing but Sister Alice for nine months.

CHAPTER 2

"O desolate world." I try this again, wetting my eyes and pinching my eyebrows together. "O, O desolate world."

Bam, bam.

"Bobbie?"

Bam, bam, bam. "Bobbie!" Mom calls. "What are you doing in there?"

"I'm getting ready, Mom."

"How come I don't hear any water running then?"

I walk over and flush the toilet.

"Are you making faces in front of the mirror, Bobbie? Because if that's what you are doing, I want you to stop it. You're going to be late for school."

"I'm all ready except for my bangs, Mom. There is something wrong with them, and I'm trying to fix them. I've wet them down and dried them. Now I look even weirder." As I say this, I think about opening the medicine cabinet, taking the cuticle sissors out, and lopping off my bangs right at the start of my forehead. How would that look? I take my towel and push my bangs off my face, flattening them against the rest of my hair. Is my forehead too big for this style?

"No one is going to notice your bangs, dear," Mom calls through the door.

Rhhwwooooooooo.

"Bobbie, is that the hair dryer? Honestly, you need to leave if you want to walk to school."

One last time I look in the mirror. America, are you tired of your bangs? Then I open the door. "Mom, I feel sick."

"You're fine. Are you sure you don't want me to drive you and your sister to school?"

"No."

"Elissa can't walk very fast."

"I know."

"You have to hold her hand across the intersection."

"I will."

"Traffic is especially heavy now with that bridge blocked off—"

"Mom, I'm twelve. I'll take care of it."

She sighs, reaches around the wall, and clicks off the bathroom light.

Down the sloping frontage road Elissa and I walk. I'm watching my feet because I like to do this when I'm wearing new shoes. Elissa is carrying my big canvas backpack for me. I hitched it right over her shoulders, on top of her own pink shiny vinyl one with the Barbies painted on the front. I told her it would be a good idea to practice carrying something heavier than just her own backpack so she'd get in shape for the walks to and from school.

It's embarrassing walking together; we're wearing the same outfit. Every girl in first through sixth grade at Saint Francis wears the same thing: plaid jumper, white blouse, navy blue sweater. In warm weather we wear white or navy short socks. In cold weather we wear white or navy tights. There are no substitutions. You can pick out your own shoes. That's it. One day last year I wore polka-dot socks, and the principal wrote a note home to my parents. Mom was understanding because all my school socks were in the wash. She said it was better in this instance to violate school policy than wear dirty socks.

It's seventy degrees out this morning, sweater and short sock weather. The sun is low in the sky, and there are layers of color surrounding it, pink and white and purple-brown, like Neapolitan ice cream. If it weren't for school, it would be a nice day for a walk.

I twirl, and the pleats on my jumper flare out. Elissa copies me, and she falls.

"It's okay, Elissa." I reach down and help her up.

"I have to go home and get a Band-Aid," she whimpers. She looks at the scratch on her knee. Her lip is quivering. She's staring at that scratch as if it were open to her bone.

"It's not even bleeding, Elissa."

"I *have* to go home. I *have* to have a Band-Aid."

I run down the grassy edge of the road, pick a sumac leaf, lick it, and slap it on her knee.

"Ow!"

11

"There's your Band-Aid, Elissa."

Elissa walks, and the leaf falls off. She starts crying again. She starts limping.

"All right, Elissa, get on my back."

I carry Elissa down the frontage road, across Highway 101, over the gas station hoses—*ding, ding*—and dump her in front of the golden arches sign. Then I dig in my pocket and offer her an old token from the roller rink if she will walk the rest of the way. Plus I offer to carry my own backpack.

Elissa looks at her knee and makes that awful face.

I buy her a large pop.

By the time we get to the dry cleaner's Elissa is finished with her pop. "Keep sucking on the straw."

"How much longer?" Elissa asks. We're in front of an old person's house. He's out raking his yard. I wave to him. Old people like that. *"Bobbie,"* Elissa says, "I said, How much longer?"

"One more block, Elissa."

"I have to go the bathroom, Bobbie."

"My name is Marie, not Bobbie. And soon, child. Soon we will reach our destination. Don't rush our awful destiny."

When I'm in a bad situation, it makes me feel better to think of a worse one. What could be a worse situation than facing sixth grade without your best friend? As we passed the funeral home, it came to me. I thought of this old movie I once saw when I was home sick. The

12

people in France were mad about the kinds of rulers they had. They got so mad that they decided to take over the country and chop off their queen's head. So I'm tucking my ponytail inside my blouse and pretending I'm being pulled in a cart. I'm Marie, the queen.

The street patrols (a fancy name for fifth- and sixth-grade kids who hold out stop-and-go flags) at the corner of Broadway are gone. Saint Francis is across the street in a butterscotch brick building. A tall fence surrounds the place. The parking lot, which is also the playground, is empty. There are no buses or kids. Either we're late, or everyone in the whole school got here early.

Pulling my ponytail out of my blouse, I announce: "I will never see the light of day again. My beautiful milky white neck will be rent in two. Farewell, France. Farewell, world."

"It scares me when you talk like that," Elissa says.

"Run with me, child." I tell her.

She looks at me with a blank face.

"Come on!"

Paper kites decorate the door frame of Sister Mary's first-grade room. Kids' names and their birthdays are written on the tails. "Look, Elissa, there's your kite." I point this out because I think it will give her a thrill. But Elissa looks as if she is going to cry.

Inside the first-grade room it smells like color crayons. All the kids are twisted back in their seats, staring at us. I feel like sticking my tongue out at each of them, but I don't because Sister Mary is walking toward us, wearing her big first-day-of-school smile. Elissa grabs the skirt of my jumper and tugs.

"What?"

"I told you I have to go to the bathroom," she whispers back. "Bad."

I glance at the clock above the pencil sharpener. Two minutes until the second bell rings.

"You must be Elissa," Sister Mary says in this real sweet voice.

Elissa nods.

Sister Mary bends down, hands on her knees. Her straight, shiny hair falls forward, and her small, silver cross swings on its chain. She smells sugary. "How nice that your big sister brought you here, Elissa."

"Elissa needs to use the bathroom, Sister Mary." It wasn't proper to blurt it out. I know that. But I had to. She's my sister, and she still wets her bed at night. No one forgets a kid who has an accident in school.

"Go ahead, Elissa," Sister Mary says. "You know where it is."

"Pick you up later, Elissa," I call. "Bye, Sister Mary."

Running, I take the stairs by twos. They're empty.

All the students must already be at their desks, talking and arranging their school supplies.

At the top of the stairs I slow down. The sun is pouring through the window in dusty streams. I crouch down and look at the cars going by on the street and

14

think of the places I could go if I were sixteen and had a car. Then the bell rings.

"No running!" my last year's teacher calls as I sprint past her room.

I can't stop. If I keep going, I can make it to the sixth-grade room before the bell has stopped ringing.

The door to my room is closed. I crank the knob hard and push. The door springs open and slams against the rubber stopper screwed into the wall. The glass on the door rattles like crazy. Whoops.

Sister Alice, standing at the blackboard, closes her eyes and wrinkles her lips as if she's just taken a whiff of something awful. She points to the empty desk.

People giggle.

I head for my seat, taking the shortcut between desks rather than going to the front of the room by Sister and walking down the wide aisle.

I squeeze past Beverly Johnson, whose chair is tilted back. Beverly can wiggle her ears. She likes to sit in class with her eyelids inside out. "Hi, Bev."

"Hi, Bobbie."

I go behind Brian Brockton. Brian always has chapped lips. He likes to draw on himself. "Hi, Brockton."

"Hi, Callahan."

Billie Cross: only boy in the class with a mustache. "Hi, Billie."

"Hi."

Sally Rutgers: pretty and popular. "Sal, hi."

"Hi, Bobbie."

I sit down—yuck—right in front of Steven Walker. Steven is a mean boy who likes to stick out his foot and trip people for a good time.

"I'm glad you're here, Roberta," Sister says to me, "but I do not tolerate tardiness. By the way, this is the last time you will be allowed to greet your friends after the second bell has rung. And while we are on the business of rules, I must tell you, that if you wish to wear that piece of jewelry, you cannot clang it against your desk. That's a pretty charm bracelet, Roberta Jean, but it is noisy and therefore potentially distracting. Please be courteous. Mr. Peedy," she says, turning toward Walter, "I, too, am a Vikings fan. But I do not advertise that fact in class. Nor will you. Remove that hat and keep it in the cloak closet."

"Sister," Steven Walker calls out. His hand is high in the air.

"What is it?" Sister says.

"Excuse me, but I can't hear you very well. Maybe if Roberta took her bracelet off, then I could hear you better."

"Or perhaps I should move you to the front of the room, Steven?" Sister says.

"No," Walker says. "I guess I can hear okay."

"No gum chewing," Sister announces. She strolls past my desk and stops at Steven's desk, where she holds out her hand. Steven pulls the gum out of his mouth and puts it in Sister's palm. Sister walks to the wastebasket and shakes her hand two or three times before the wad falls off into the garbage. "No toys. None of those blinking machines. Put it away, Harold."

"It's not a toy, Sister," Harold tells her. "It's my calculator."

"That includes calculators, Harold. There are people in the world who cannot add or subtract without pushing buttons on a box. You, Harold, will not be one of them. All my students become proficient with an ancient tool called the pencil. Brian, go to the lavatory and scrub those pictures off your arms."

Sister walks to the board and starts writing. She is done with the rules. At least I think she's done. Maybe someone will raise an eyebrow, and Sister can tell that person, "Uh-uh, no, keep it down."

Karen James, sitting in front of me, turns around quickly and says, "Hi." Karen lives in my neighborhood. People sometimes whisper that she is slow.

"Kind of late there, stretch," Steven Walker says with a sneer.

"Did I say you could visit?" Sister whirls around and faces the class. Her long navy blue skirt whirls, too.

In the movies and on TV nuns wear habits. But none of the nuns I know do. They wear regular clothes. I have an aunt who is a nun and she wears Bermuda shorts. I'm not kidding. Last summer we had a family reunion and Aunt Helen showed up in a sweatshirt and shorts. And can she slug a softball!

I can't imagine Sister Alice slugging a softball. She wouldn't be caught dead in a sweatshirt. Shorts? No.

Her skirts are always down to her ankles. I'll never see her legs. You can bet your life on that.

"Please remove your outerwear, Roberta Jean. We are ready to begin today's lesson."

Lesson! You don't do any work on the first day of school. Everyone knows that. I walk to the cloak closet and hang my backpack on a hook.

"Nice going, Row-bert-ta," Steven Walker whispers when I sit back down. He leans forward when Sister isn't looking and blows hard into the back of my hair. "Have some germs, Row-berta Jean. Blue Jeans. Jeanie-weanie. Whatja do over the summer? Take growth hormones?"

"Sit back in your seat, Mr. Walker," Sister says. "Class," she says, changing her voice entirely, "rise for prayer."

Sister's eyes close, and the skin between her almost invisible eyebrows pinches to a deep line. When we finish the prayer, she opens her eyes and says, "It is now time to ask God for our special intentions."

No one says anything, but silently in my heart I ask God to make me shorter. I've been asking this for some time.

After we sit down, Sister walks to her desk and picks up a black vinyl folder. Turning away from us, digging in a side pocket, she pulls out a red pen. Then abruptly she turns and faces the windows. Screwing up her face, she marches over and pulls down two shades. She walks back to her desk and—*ting*—pushes the button of a little silver bell. "What is all this talking going on? If any of you have something to say, say it to the entire class. Katherine Marie?"

"I wasn't talking, Sister."

We all swivel in our seats to look at Katherine.

"I know you weren't, Katherine," Sister says. "I am taking attendance."

Poor Katherine. Someone must have scared her when she was little, and she has never gotten over it. Last year Katherine was nominated Student of the Year by our teacher, Mrs. Cotts. Katherine got to wear a dress to school. She got to wear nylons. "Perfect attendance," Mrs. Cotts said, listing Katherine's winning qualities from the lectern. "Hands her work in on time, demonstrates cooperative behavior on the playground, never talks out of turn." Never talks at all, she should have said.

"Oh," Katherine squeaks. "I'm here."

"Speak up, Katherine Marie," Sister says.

Katherine looks at her desk and nods yes.

Sister doesn't know Katherine very well. She *was* speaking up. People as shy as Katherine Anderson make me want to talk for them. Or sneak up behind them and shout, "Boo!," depending on what kind of mood I'm in.

"Samuel Hamel," Sister calls.

My heart kicks when she says his name.

"Here," he answers.

"Good, Samuel," Sister says. "I didn't think you were paying attention. No middle name, Samuel?"

"No," Sam answers.

Samuel Hamel. What's the matter with those parents

19

of his? Didn't they consider rhymes when they named him? Of course, he gets called Sam the Ham.

"Roberta Jean Callahan."

"That's Bobbie, Sister."

"Pardon me?" Sister says.

"No one calls me Roberta anymore. Everyone calls me Bobbie."

"Roberta Jean is a lovely name," Sister tells me.

Well, so what? Who cares about that? But all right, fine, if Sister is in love with names, let her call me Roberta Jean. She calls all the other kids by their *real* names. Except if you have a double last name. Boy, she hates those. If you have one of those hyphenated mother-father combination names, she drops one half. Roberta Jean Callahan, I'll admit to it. I open my mouth to speak, and I burp.

The kids start laughing.

I didn't mean to burp.

The room is shaking with laughter. It seems that way.

It would be different if I were trying to burp. That might be funny. I wasn't trying to.

Sister stares at me. Then she lifts her head and looks around at the rest of the class. "Stop it. You've heard someone burp before."

Late that afternoon I watch the sun sink behind the trees from inside my dog's cedar house. It's a big house; the dog and I can sit up straight with a two-inch clearance from our heads to the roof. Dad built the house thinking we were going to get two dogs, but when Mom and I walked in with Hannah, a full-grown Newfoundland that we picked up at the pound, Dad said, "No way. One horse is enough."

I'm looking out the door. The sun is spreading across the sky, melting into butter. Pretty soon the trees will drop their leaves, and the ground all around Hannah's house will be brown and crunchy. But right now the leaves are soft, soft enough to fold and string into a chain. I've made two crowns. One for me and one for Hannah.

"Guinevere, I love you."

Hannah stares at me.

"I'll always love you."

Hannah wipes her tongue across my face.

"King Arthur," I say to myself, "try to understand."

Hannah groans, lies down, and starts chewing a sore on her foot. Her leaf crown falls to the floor.

I pick it up and put it back on her head. I lie down next to her. "Charlotte Hansen wouldn't have laughed at me today, I can tell you that, Guinevere."

Hannah's eyes are closed.

"Best friends are like that. They don't make fun of you. Even if everyone else is making fun of you."

Hannah is sleeping.

I lift up her ear. "Guinevere, did you hear what I said?"

Dear Charlotte Hansen in Pittsburgh,

I'm so tired that I might faint or die, but I wanted
to write to you first. How are you? I'm bad. It's a
black year for me, Charlotte. And it's not just
because you're not here. It's also Sister Alice.
She's so strict it's not even funny.

Right now I'm doing homework. Homework
on a Saturday. Can you believe it? Friday Harold
raised his hand and told Sister that all last year
we were never assigned homework on the
weekend. "How unfortunate," she said.

Monday we're having a geography test. I bet
we're the only class in the nation that has had
three big tests in the first two weeks of school.

Sister's tests are hard. Each kid in our class is
given a different test. It's true. She must have
nothing better to do than make up this stuff. And
it's not fair. My questions are a lot harder than
other kids' questions. On our history test last
week, Karen James's essay questions were: "What
President negotiated the Louisiana Purchase, and
why?" My questions were: "What impact did the
Louisiana Purchase have on frontier America?
What did the purchase mean to Jefferson's
administration? What does the purchase mean to
you and succeeding generations of Americans?" Of
course, I had to explain all three answers with
complete sentences. If you don't use complete

22

sentences, Sister takes points off your grade. She also takes points off for not putting your name where you're supposed to, poor sentence structure, and sloppy penmanship. She's taken points off every one of my tests for slanting my handwriting in the wrong direction.

Mom says things will get better, it just takes time. Dad says I'm all ready if they decide to send me to a military school for junior high. Ha-ha, Dad.

I could write more, but I'm in the bathroom pretending I'm a pioneer girl. The pioneer girl in the book I read wrote her letters in a woodshed. I don't have to tell you we don't have one of those. Anyway, my parents don't understand the importance of props. They'd get mad if they knew I was burning a candle in here. I'm going to blow it out now and spray Gramma's Jean Naté around.

One last thing. Something good did happen to me this week. Sam bumped into me. On purpose. Do I like him? I'm not sure. First I have to find out if he likes me. What I know is that when I grow up, I'm not marrying any of the boys in my class. I'm moving to New York. Being an actress is a tough life, Charlotte. I can't be tied down.

Love,
Bobbie

CHAPTER 3

I'm sitting on the ledge of my window, two stories off the ground. My head is under the eaves; my legs are dangling; my heels are scraping stucco. The sun has spent the day warming things up. So my sweater is off, tied around my waist. My tights are in a ball on the floor.

I'm watching leaves fall. I've missed out on a bunch of watching days already. Tons of leaves have fallen. They're dead on the ground, brown as potatoes. The ones on the trees are loaded with color, and the branches hold and wave them like pretty paper napkins.

A big wind—shake, shake—there they go. Floating, they slide back and forth across the sky, until they drop to the ground.

The air outside is soaked with the smell of fresh tar. A new surface was laid on the road out front, and from my window, high up here, I can see it, black and shining. Sewer and city water came through, and for a whole two weeks the street was torn up. This meant that after five o'clock, when the workers went home, I got to go exploring. I was in Peru, wandering around in the crack of an earthquake. . . . Help me! I was Curdie in the goblins' underground headquarters, trying to save the princess. (Girl or boy, I always take the best part.) I was a hermit, living on slugs, and that's when I found it, an unusually large black and yellow snake.

"Right, Desdemona?" I poke my head back inside and look over at my ten-gallon aquarium.

Snakes never answer. They don't even look up when you call their names. Snakes are dumb. Actually, though, I'm getting attached to her, or him. (How do you tell?) I get attached to almost any animal.

The aquarium was the only thing I could think of to put Desdemona in. I had to transfer Ozzie and Harriet, my two goldfish, to a large salad bowl. We haven't had company in a while, so Mom hasn't missed the bowl. And she hasn't found out about the snake because she doesn't like to come in my room. Neither does my dad. They say they're afraid of what they'll find. Pretty soon I'm going to put the aquarium in my closet. That way Desdemona can pretend she's hibernating.

"Land sakes, girl! What are you doing hanging out that window?"

I turn and look over my shoulder. Gramma is standing in the doorway, holding a mixing spoon caked with cookie dough. "It's okay, Gramma. I do it all the time."

"Not while I'm responsible for you, you don't. Good grief, you could fall and crack your skull open."

"That won't happen."

"Get down."

I duck my head back inside, brace myself against the window frame, throw my legs over the sill, and jump to the floor.

Gramma walks over and hands me the spoon. "You got the bowl last time. Elissa gets it this time. Fair is fair. After this last batch is done"—she glances at her watch—"we're going out."

"Where?"

"Somewhere. I want to take the convertible for its last spin. I can tell by my knees and elbows it's going to be an early winter."

"Sorry, Gram, I don't feel like it."

"I'm old, and I can't hear you," she says, smoothing the folds in her apron. "Besides, it's not good for a young girl to spend so much time brooding in her room. Fresh air cures anything. Do you like this color?" Gramma bunches up the curly ends of her reddish pink hair. "Sylvia said it suits me."

I lick my spoon, deciding how to get out of this— both the errand and the hair question—without hurting Gram's feelings.

"We can drop your sister off at Fanny's house," Gramma says, turning to leave. "It'll be just you and me and Big Blue."

"I have homework to do, Gram. Maybe tomorrow."

"Since when do you do homework on a Friday? Shut that window, and bring a jacket. How are you, snake?"

*　*　*

Highway 12 going east toward downtown Minneapolis is under construction. Major construction. Sunburned guys in hard hats are all over the place. Mountains of dirt divide one side of the highway from the other. Giant cranes swing hooks. Vacant lots sit where homes used to be, and store windows are so close to the shoulder of the road you could throw rocks from your car and smash them.

Because of the noise and road dust, the top is up on the convertible, but Gramma, probably out of habit, talks loud anyway. "Say what you will about Henry Ford, Bobbie girl, the automobile is the best invention ever made. Aren't you glad you came along now?" We swerve and I lean and Saint Christopher dangles by a blue ribbon tied to the mirror.

"I guess so."

The tunnel on Interstate 94 appears, and Gramma screams, "Make your wish, Bobbie baby!"

The tunnel is dark and tiled like a huge bathroom. I hold my breath and wish that a Hollywood talent scout would discover me early. *Pwahhh*, we're out again. Light bombs the windshield. "Why are we going this way, anyway, Gram?"

"I want to see the old place again," Gramma says, staring into the traffic. "Say good-bye to it. Your grandfather built that house, you know."

"I know. What do you mean, good-bye?"

"Good-bye. Hello, good-bye. Just in case I don't get over that way again."

We turn off on Hiawatha Avenue. Scrubby bushes and strip malls line the road. We pass the big railroad yard and the dog chow factory that smells like peanut butter. Gray warehouses; one stoplight after another.

Red light, we wait. Some fat lady, one car over, is applying makeup in front of her rearview mirror. Her baby in the back is strapped in a car seat and bawling, turning its sweaty head from side to side. I look at it and pretend I'm bawling, too. I've found from baby-sitting that this sometimes helps kids stop crying. It's my shock therapy. But it doesn't work with this kid. The light turns green, and we drive on.

Some stores become familiar now, the names I couldn't have told you. It's been six years since Grandpa died, and four years since Gramma sold her house and moved in with us. Dad insisted. Mom was for it. Gramma said, "No, no," over a lot of Sunday ham dinners. "I'm fine here, Charles. I like my little house." Gramma changed her mind when her next-door neighbor, Ima Swanson, went into a nursing home. "I don't want to lose my mind, too, living here alone."

Over the cream stone bridge we go by the yellow house that was once a zoo where a lion escaped (if you can believe Gramma), make the second right, around the block, and pull up to the curb in front of Gram's house.

Gram turns off the car but doesn't get out. Hands flat against the steering wheel, she leans over toward my window and looks out. A red string of bells hangs down from her old front door. The chocolate brown shutters are gone, and because of the difference in the color of paint underneath them, it looks as if they left their shadow. The bushes are bigger. There aren't any cats sleeping on the steps.

"Well," Gram, says. She picks up her gloves and purse and gets out.

Well? Is that all? Messy bushes, the house needs shutters, and I don't know what about those bells. I get out of the car.

"Lock it," Gram says. She is getting situated. She pushes up the strap of her purse to her elbow, feels the bobby pins that hold her hairnet, puts on one glove, holds the other glove.

"Remember me, creek?" I shout. "*House*! Remember me?"

Gramma starts walking.

I stare at the back of her blue quilted coat. What's the hurry? If I were Gram, I'd be looking the place over. I'd peek in a window. I'd step up to the door and ring the bell to see if anyone were home. If someone were home and didn't look too creepy, I'd ask to use the bathroom. You can tell a lot about people by looking at their bathrooms, especially if you open their medicine chest. "Gram, wait up."

She stops and turns, and when I reach her, she locks her arm in mine. I guess it's okay if we walk around connected this way since it's not my neighborhood.

Strolling side by side, I think about how tall I am and how short Gram is. The top of her head just meets the top of my shoulder, and that's including her poofy hairstyle. She is barely five feet, and pudgy. Or at least I always thought of her as pudgy: lots of fat and strong bones filled with gravy. But today she seems . . . I don't know . . . kind of fragile. Her back has a slight hump that I notice now as if it's some other grandma's hump. I could snap and break the arm I'm holding, really it feels that way, and for the first time I notice Gram has cheekbones.

The sun has slid away, and the air is cool. We walk along by smoky dark-time light. When we reach the end of the block, Gram says, "Crazy Ethel." We turn the corner. I know what comes next, and I say the words to myself: Met her husband in the nuthouse.

"Met her husband, Donald, in the nuthouse," Gram says, and pokes me with her pointer finger. "Never a pot so crooked that you can't find a lid."

We passed Crazy Ethel's house a long way back. It was the dark green one next to Gram's with the twenty-seven cuckoo clocks. I bet Ethel isn't living there any-more because the cats are gone, the ones that used to sleep on Gramma's steps.

"Clipped coupons all day long," Gramma says. "For-ever entering some dumb contest. Nearly choked me one time. Oh, yes. Claimed I was after Donald. After that I never let her in the house. I couldn't. I kept my door hooked and would talk to her through the screen. It's a pity. I wonder what ever became of that woman."

Each house on the block Gramma comments on, starting from Crazy Ethel's and on down the street. "This is Eldridge's place. Or at least it used to be. Widowed at the age of forty. Never did remarry. Not a bad-looking man either. The baker lived in that brick house. After he retired, he used to do my windows. Course, I paid him. Right here"—Gramma stops and makes a circle with her arms high above her head—"there used to be a big spreading elm." She pulls my sleeve and whispers, "Kissed Cullie under that tree many a summer evening. Oh, you might not think I was ever young, but I was. Quite a looker, too, if I must say so myself."

"Gram-ma."

"It's the truth. And I was taller. Looked a lot like my granddaughter."

Gramma winks, straightens her spine, hooks her arm in mine, and we walk on down the alley.

"How that blind lady ever took care of her house and yard and *that* dog, I'll never know. Chew-chew or Pooh-pooh his name was. Ugliest piece of ragamuffin dog you've ever seen."

We pass the blue house.

"Now Marian found Curtis dead in a lawn chair one afternoon on that very porch. Middle of the day it was. Can you imagine? I despise lawn ornaments, don't you?

31

I nursed their Tommy boy all one night when he had the German measles. I was the only one on the block who had ever been to nursing school. They called on me for everything. Gave enemas, you name it."

"Enemas! Ick!"

Gramma laughs and makes a fist and pretends to squirt something out of it.

We reach the back of her house, and her face changes. She touches my arm, the one that's bent around her arm, with the glove she's holding. We stand still in the alley.

"Heh, the garden is gone." I hadn't noticed it at first. But I should have. The garden took up half the backyard.

"Yup," Gramma says. She says it real soft and doesn't look in my face.

When we used to visit Gram, I'd go in the backyard while Mom and Dad and Gram were talking in the house. I'd do stupid stuff like play with the hose for two hours or chase ants up the walk. Looking at her backyard now, I feel the same way I feel when summer ends.

Gramma isn't saying anything about anything. She's just looking.

Finally she says, "That house looked better with shutters." Then she lifts her arm and swats the air as if she's telling someone to go on, go away.

We walk around the block, get in the car, and drive home.

Dear Charlotte Hansen in Pittsburgh,

What do you think about getting old? I don't mean twenty. I mean *real* old.

I never thought my gramma would get old. Not old like other old people. But lately she's been getting tired easily. It's weird because before, Gramma always said she never got tired. (She also never got hot or cold.) But it's not true. Gramma has been taking naps. She gets out of breath.

The picture I drew you at the bottom of this letter is supposed to be my mouth. Last week I got braces on my teeth. At first I couldn't talk right. Now that's better, and my biggest problem is that when I eat, I get food stuck between my wires. I've been practicing smiling with my mouth closed. Next Thursday is school pictures.

Charlotte, in your last letter you didn't talk about any of your friends. Have you made any friends? Maybe it's too soon. I don't know because I've never moved.

Lately I've been hanging around with Karen James. Yesterday we walked along the railroad tracks and threw rocks at telephone poles. You can do this kind of junk with Karen and not feel dumb.

I suppose you think it's funny that I'm hanging

around with Karen. The reason I am is that all the other girls at school are pretty much paired or tripled up. You know what I mean, they do certain stuff with certain people, and that's it. Beverly always invites Sally to her house. Katherine invites Christina. Last year it was you and me. Being most people think Karen is a geek, she didn't have anyone to hang around with. I didn't either.

School is the same. Sister wrote a note home to my parents. She told them I needed to work on my attitude. Dad read the letter out loud to me, and he made mad faces the whole time. Mom was pretty disappointed, too.

And get this. The other day I saw Sister riding a bike through my neighborhood (yes, a bike). I bet she spies on her students.

> G. F. N. (Good-bye for now)
> Bobbie

P.S. Sam asked to use my pencil the other day. I'm sure he had one of his own.

CHAPTER 4

When I see the Buick driving down the frontage road, I know I'm in trouble.

"Stop dawdling!" Dad screams out the passenger-side window. "You've got fifteen minutes to get to school."

"It's all her fault, Dad," Elissa yells back. "She made me lie down in the grass, and now I'm all dirty."

Dad pounds his fist once on the steering wheel. "I don't care whose fault it is. Get going!" His car kicks up gravel on the shoulder of the road and speeds away.

"It's all your fault," Elissa says.

"Be quiet, Elissa. Baby Moses never carried on like this."

"I'm all dirty."

"I gave you the lead role, Elissa. What do you want? Do you want to be Miriam?"

"I don't want to be in your stupid plays, Bobbie."

"Productions. How many times do I have to say it? *Productions*." I brush off her back, swing her backpack over my shoulder, take her hand, and practically pull her off the frontage road and across the highway. We're in a hurry now.

Blinng! The bell mounted on the outside of the school shakes as we pass through the opening someone cut in the fence.

"We're late!" Elissa shrieks. "I told you. I didn't want to stop. I wanted to go right to school like Mom said. You made me stop, Bobbie. You made me."

"Look at the window, Elissa. Kids are on the landing. It's only the first bell."

"My teacher likes us to be in our desks at the first bell."

"She likes you to be. You don't have to be."

"I don't want her to get mad at me."

"She won't get mad, Elissa. You're in first grade. Go in there now, and she won't say a thing."

Elissa doesn't move. She stands and looks at the outside of the school and sniffs, taking in breaths that sound as if they're going up a stairs in her nose.

"Look, Elissa, I'll get a pink slip if *I'm* late. *I'll* get detention. Do you want me to get in trouble and get detention? Nothing's going to happen to you."

"The kids will see me crying, Bobbie."

I pull my sweater up over my hand and wipe her face. "There."

"Can't you come with me?" she asks.

The second bell rings by the time we get to the first-grade door. Sister Mary is standing with a book open. "I'm so glad you're here, Elissa," she says.

I nudge Elissa, who is halfway hiding behind me.

She peeks out, lifts her chin, and opens her mouth like she's getting her throat checked. "I lost my tooth last night, Sister Mary. See?"

"Wuf-da!" Sister Mary says, sucking in a big breath.

Elissa jumps up and claps. "I get a certificate!" (And my parents say *I'm* moody.)

"Yes, you do," Sister Mary says. "A big yellow one with a star. I'm going to my desk right this minute and make it out."

Elissa takes my hand again. Sister Mary walks to her closet and pulls a sheet of yellow construction paper from a stack on a shelf. At her desk she takes the top off a black Magic Marker and writes—with a squeaking noise, saying the words out loud—"Elissa Callahan lost her right front tooth on October 14. Boys and girls?" She shows the class.

"You forgot the star!" a little kid in the front row with two new beaver teeth says.

"So I did," Sister Mary says. "Where do you want it, Elissa?"

Elissa walks over to Sister Mary's desk and points.

Sister Mary looks toward me and nods. You can go, she means. Everything is fine.

Everything is fine except that I'm going to get detention. I turn and walk to the office.

"Mr. Williams?"

Mr. Williams, our principal, looks up from his desk. "I need a late pass."

He drops his pencil, sits back, and folds his arms. "You're late again?"

"I sort of got tied up."

"Come on, Bobbie. I know better than that." He gets up and walks over to the file cabinet in a corner of his office. "Sit down," he tells me. Then he opens the middle drawer and pulls out a folder. "One, two, three times you've been tardy this year. And we're not even into the fifth week of school. What's going on with you?"

I shrug my shoulders.

Mr. Williams closes the file drawer with his hip and slaps the folder down on his desk. He walks over to the orange vinyl chair I'm sitting on. "We're friends," he says.

Only since last spring have we been friends. Last spring Mr. Williams went to some kind of long meeting in California. He came back to school wearing open-collar shirts and plain old kick-around pants, instead of the dark suits he used to wear. He painted his office yellow, said he wanted it to look cheery like the sun. It looks nothing like the sun. It looks as if someone smeared mustard all over the walls.

"Problems at home, Bobbie?" he asks, putting his hands on either side of the armrests.

"No."

"Boy trouble?"

"No."

"Well?"

I shrug my shoulders again. Mr. Williams has a burst of veins on each side of his wide nose. He has a mole with hair growing out of it on his chin. His breath smells like coffee.

"All last year you never got detention."

"Last year I had Mrs. Cotts for a teacher. She didn't care if I was late. She said the first fifteen minutes of school were free time anyway."

"It's a new year this year. Remember?" Mr. Williams sounds mad when he says this. I guess sometimes he forgets his new self and acts like his old self.

I nod.

"I like you, Bobbie," Mr. Williams says, suddenly smiling. "You're a good kid. Basically. You don't want to get branded as a troublemaker, do you?"

"No."

"Okay, then," he says, patting me on the shoulder. "Okay. Buckle down. Okay? Get to school on time."

"Does that mean I don't get detention?"

Mr. Williams goes around to the other side of his desk, opens a drawer, and pulls out a pink pad with a blue binding. He writes, rips off the sheet of paper, and hands it to me. "No. You still get detention. Would it be fair to the other students if I made exceptions to the rule just for you?"

Slowly I walk to my classroom. Every other green and gray linoleum square I step on. The hall bulletin board has last year's blue ribbon for the spelling bee tacked to it. The showcase has a model town made out of sugar

39

cubes. Step green, step gray . . . the first graders are finger painting. Elissa is a mess.

Up the gritty stairs to the second floor I go, stopping and kneeling in front of the landing window. Outside, the swings move in the wind as if they're full of invisible kids. A motorcycle, a taxicab, cars, a city bus go by. And there, along the sidewalk, on the street side of the chain-link fence, is Raymond.

Raymond is a homeless guy. Most of the day he walks around the streets of our town. I mean I guess that's what he does since every time I see him that's what he is doing. Sometimes he does hitchhike. But I've never seen anyone pick him up, so I don't know if he ever really goes places in cars.

Where are you going now, Raymond? And what are you thinking? Do you miss a bed? Do you ever wish you got mail?

Getting up, I walk straight to the second-floor drinking fountain. Then I decide I had better get to my class.

"Hello there, Bette Davis," a voice calls as I walk by the janitor's closet.

"Hi, Mr. George."

"Late, kiddo?"

I shake my head yes.

He shakes his head in the opposite direction while he wrings out his mop.

Mr. George has been the janitor at Saint Francis for as long as I've been here. He has skin the color of wheat bread, a black mustache, and stubs, but no beard. He's always calling me by some famous actress's name. I think it's part of his inspirational program for me. Once when I was sent out in hall, he told me he had been in reform school. He told me this leaning on his broom with his eyebrows lifted as if to say: So you see, be careful. Mr. George, a juvenile delinquent—it's the best secret anyone has ever told me.

The rippled window on my classroom door rattles, and the kids whisper and poke one another as I walk in.

Sister studies the pass I hand her. She glances at the clock. She looks at me. She looks again at the pass. "I don't believe it takes seven minutes to walk from the office to our room. But I'll let that one go, Roberta. You realize this is your fourth tardy mark?"

"Yes."

"That means detention," she says.

Sister knows I know what it means.

"I'll call your parents and tell them you'll be staying after school, Roberta. Someone will need to come and pick up your sister. Take your seat. And don't drag your shoes across the floor."

I go to my desk.

"Roberta?" Sister says after I've sat down.

"What?"

"We were just talking about spiritual narcissism. Do you know what that means?"

"No."

Sister marches to the blackboard and writes: "ME, ME,

41

ME." She sets the chalk on the ledge, brushes off her hands, turns around. "We live in the 'me' times, class. As a society we want only what feels good for us, never mind our neighbor. This is not as it should be. Sit up straight in your seat, Mr. Walker. Knees forward. Thank you. More than five billion people walk the face of this earth. It is our job, it is everyone's job, to elevate the station of the masses." Sister pushes up with her hands as if she's opening a stuck window.

My parents are going to be really mad that I got detention.

"Roberta? Are you listening?"

"Fa-la-la-la-la-la-la-a-a." As Sister sings, she caresses the stiff white collar covering her throat.

It's second hour, music, and today it's being held in the church balcony. I hate music. But I *love* the balcony.

From the balcony the priest and altar boys are miniatures. The organ is a toy.

There is no ceiling over the balcony; the walls just keep going up, getting narrower and narrower until they bend into the bell tower of the steeple. Four stained glass windows are way the heck up there, too. Does Mr. George have to clean these? I don't know.

"Hymnals are not comic books, Mr. Peedy," Sister says. She clops across the wooden floor to the piano.

Walter looks up, squinting over his glasses and under his bangs. He doesn't understand.

Sister has arranged the seats by singing ability. She

didn't tell us this, but I just know that the good singers are in the back so their voices carry and drown out the not-so-hot ones. This is why I don't like music. I'm second row from the front, right next to Walter. The next nearest girl is three rows back.

"I *said*, Mr. Peedy, hymnals are not comic books." Sister's arms are crossed. One chunk heel is out to the side.

"Take your hymnal off your knees, Walter," I whisper.

Walter picks up his hymnal. His chubby finger follows the notes.

"Articulate," Sister tells us. Her shoes are back together. Her tongue taps her teeth. "Sing loud, people," she says. "Remember, we are singing to the Lord."

God may be disappointed in me. I sing soft, so no one can hear my off pitch, and dance the toes of my shoes in the colored light coming down from the steeple.

Third hour is social studies, and Sister is mad. She is also out of breath. We just got finished with music, and we're back in our room. To get here, we had to climb down two flights of stairs from the balcony to the church basement. Then we had to pass through the echoing tunnel—"O,o,o, Boo,oo,oo, Heh,heh,heh"—to the school lunchroom, where we walked in a straight line *with our mouths closed*, before we climbed two more flights of stairs to our classroom.

"You are all getting red check marks by your names

43

for that immature behavior through the tunnel," Sister tells us. She closes the door and strides to her desk. She opens a drawer, finds her attendance book, and shows us the red pen.

I take out my own pen, neon with purple ink, and a piece of paper.

"Did I say it was time for art?" Sister asks me.

I put the paper back in my desk. But I keep the pen in my lap. While Sister is busy with her attendance book, I draw on the top of my desk. Wetting my finger, I smear the little man I drew and rub my hand in the ink. My palm is purple. I tap on Karen's shoulder to show her. She doesn't turn around.

I feel like getting up and walking around. I feel like opening my mouth and yelling, "Panama Canal." I feel like winging my arms around and around and around until they fly off my shoulders. It's an hour away from lunch. After that is recess. I can't wait.

Sister puts her book back in the drawer and says, "According to the new curriculum plan, we are to devote one hour of social studies every month to Program Jut. That is an acronym—" Sister moves to the board and writes the word *acronym*. "Say it, class."

Together everyone says, "Ac-ro-nym."

"An acronym is, of course, a word formed from the intial letters of words, or parts of words," Sister says. "*JUT* is formed from the initial letters of *join us together*. Program JUT was established in the belief that if children could share their feelings, their self-esteem would increase. It's an overrated idea, in my opinion. Feelings are important, but you don't gain self-esteem by simply talking about it. You gain self-esteem by *doing*. That is why we are going to the convent this hour and making vegetable soup. This evening I will drive to Sharing and Caring Hands and deliver it. We can talk about how we feel while we're peeling potatoes.

"Oh, Roberta," Sister says. "You may go to the lavatory and wash your hands. Then you may stand in the hall for ten minutes. I saw you drawing on your desk."

Last hour is gym class.

Wheeeeet! Sister blows her whistle. "Line up with your partners," she says. "Eleven inches apart."

"Why can't we play field hockey? Tell me that."

Billie answers me by hunching up his shoulders and dropping them down. Billie is my partner.

Sister strolls across the floor in her black skirt and Keds. When she reaches the cart with the beige phonograph on top of it, she calls out to Walter, "Since Katherine is absent today, Mr. Peedy—

"What is so funny?" Sister asks.

What is so funny is that Walter has to dance with Sister. She's making us all learn to dance.

Walter walks slumped to Sister.

"Stand tall," she tells him when he reaches her.

"Everyone," she calls out, "stand tall." She rests her hand lightly on Walter's shoulder.

"Shimmying the rope would be better than this. Don't you think, Billie?"

Billie looks down at his Dock-Siders. I've known Billie since kindergarten. But he's hardly said a word to me since we started being dance partners.

Sister doesn't usually teach phys ed. Mr. Brumble does. But he broke his leg playing softball.

It happened at school. Mr. Brumble was running toward home plate when Harold, the pitcher, threw the ball to Sally, our catcher. Brumble slid. Sally tagged him out. Everyone on our team cheered. We kept cheering until we realized Mr. Brumble wasn't getting up.

This is embarrassing. Billie's head is only as high as my chin. "The boys will catch up to you," my dad says. When, Dad?

"Remain light on the floor," Sister calls out. "Dance on the balls of your feet." Sister lifts a corner of her skirt as she demonstrates the dance. She's wearing white crew socks with black stockings underneath.

Billie isn't even watching Sister. His hair smells like salad oil.

Gosh, do I smell? I hope I don't smell.

"Basically the waltz step is a box formation," Sister says. "*One*, two, three. *One*, two, three." She calls out the count, nodding her head, giving Walter the signals to move.

Walter is stomping his massive feet, trying to do the steps right.

"One moment, please," Sister says. She lets go of

Walter and takes a record out of an album cover. She blows on the record and sets it on the turntable.

The music starts playing, and Sister shouts, "Begin!"

Billie lifts his foot and steps on his shoe. Then he lifts his other foot and steps on his other shoe. Back and forth, back and forth, he steps on his shoes.

I stand waiting with my arms dangling. If I had a mustache like Billie, I'd shave it off. Even if I was only in sixth grade.

All the other kids are starting to dance. They're holding hands and watching each other's feet.

Beverly has Sam for a partner. Maybe this wouldn't be so bad if I had Sam for a partner. No, come to think of it, that would even be more embarrassing.

"William! Roberta!" Sister hollers. "What are you two waiting for?" Sister waltzes over with Walter to get close to us.

Tomorrow I'm going to figure out a way to get out of this. But for now I pick up Billie's limp, wet hand, put my other hand on his shoulder, and start pushing him around. He has no rhythm. Why should he lead?

The moon is pale yellow. There are no stars. Out here in the dark I listen. Clunk-clunk, a car drives over the railroad tracks. The car passes our house and lights everything up. For a second I can see my ladder perfectly.

I hope the person in the car wasn't one of our neighbors.

When Dad got home tonight, he was pretty mad. I

heard him ask, "Where is she?" from way downstairs. "You had better start coming around and waking up to reality," Dad told me. "You've got Sister for the whole year. Get used to it."

That's why I hope it wasn't one of our neighbors in that car. I'm supposed to be in my room thinking about my behavior. I figure I can think about it just as well out here.

The ladder came from the *Safety First* catalog. It's a twelve-foot-long fire escape ladder. It's made of aluminum. It folds up into a blanket box. It unfurls in seconds. (Impressed? It says all this on the box.) I'm about— looking down at the tops of the bushes—halfway up.

Use this ladder when your doorway is blocked, Dad said. He showed me how to crouch down and feel for heat under the crack of the door. He timed me while I got the ladder out from under my bed and hooked it onto the windowsill. Mom thought the whole business was silly (her exact words). "Two hundred dollars on ladders?" she said. "Let the kids jump. That's not going to kill them."

Back in my room, with the ladder folded under my bed, I pick out the fattest book on the shelf: the dictionary.

Narcissism. Number one. "Excessive admiration of self." Oh. I go over to my dresser and pick up my mirror.

"Hello, Bobbie."

"Hello."

48

"I love you."
"I love you, too."
"You're going to be a star someday."
"Big star."
"Even though you're tall."
"Very tall."
"Good night, sugar."
"Good night."

CHAPTER 5

"The trouble with Ima Swanson," Gramma says, "is that she never gave up. One warm night the old man packed his suitcase and took the train. All summer long Ima would put on her hat and go down to the station to wait for him to come home. Ima was one woman who could wear a hat and have it look like it belonged there. Here, say hello to her, Bobbie." Gramma presses down the "record" and "play" buttons on her tape recorder, cups the little microphone in her hand, and holds it near my mouth.

"Hi."

Taking back the microphone, Gramma says in a loud voice, "That was Charlie's oldest, Ima." She presses "pause" and chuckles softly. "I'll remind Ima about the spring your father cut off the tops of her prize tulips. She'll remember that."

"He never came back?"

"Who?" Gramma says, picking up her knitting needles. "Her old man? Of course not. He was doomed from the day he starting asking what life was all about. Drank gin and shaved on Sunday."

I watch Gramma's hands. Purl, hook, she knits without looking, as if it's the same as breathing.

"Much later," Gramma says, "Ima went funny in the head. But I trace the start of it back to that summer." Gramma sets her knitting inside her wicker basket and eases back in her chair. The chair creaks.

Everything in this room of Gram's is old, including Grandpa's wooden toolbox, which sits locked and polished in a corner. Gramma's room is one-half of the attic. A pocket door on the back wall of her closet leads to the rest of the attic. You can crawl around in there if you don't mind spiders. Gram says she prefers her room to other bedrooms because it has character, and she hates anything that's wishy-washy. I agree. The attic is my favorite place in the house.

I walk from Gram's desk to her bed under the skylights. Rain is beating against the roof. I take off my shoes and lie down on my stomach. You're dead if you forget to take your shoes off on Gramma's bed. Her quilt is sixty years old, made by her mother, pieced from the patches of five sisters' clothes: Sarah, Mary, Jane, Kate, and Cecilia. Gramma is Sarah. Her back is to me now, but I can hear her slow, easy talk just fine, and that is the reason why I'm up here. I love to listen to her make tapes for Mrs. Swanson.

"Remember the weekend of the peaches, Ima," Gramma says. "We had it in our heads to plant peach trees—period!—never mind the climate."

Every week Gramma sends a tape to Pleasant Valley

Nursing Home, where Mrs. Swanson lives. A couple of times Gramma has taken me there to visit. It's awful. All day long Mrs. Swanson sits tied to a chair. She wears diapers under her nightgown, and the nursing home workers have to feed her or she won't eat. Gramma says Mrs. Swanson is like a baby, and the stories on tape are her lullabies.

"It was some year that year, Ima. The soil was as dry as the chicken bones you left out on the picnic table. When—" *Click.*

The recorder is off. I turn and look at Gram. Her thin shoulders are hunched forward. "Gram? What's wrong?"

I hop off the bed. Gramma's eyes are shut.

There's sweat above her lip.

"Gram?"

"Gramma?"

She holds up her hand, meaning wait, and strains to breathe.

I run and get her purse from the closet and shake the purse out on the floor. Wallet, checkbook . . . pills. I line up the red arrow on the lid of the bottle and twist off the cap. Tablets spill all over the floor.

Gramma is holding a hand to her chest. She sees the pill and says, "Thanks," but hardly any sound comes out. Her breaths are coming hard. She takes the pill and puts it under her tongue.

"Are you okay?"

She nods her head and scrunches up her eyes. She

mumbles, "I've had these spells for years. It was that chicken. That greasy chicken."

"You're pale, Gramma."

Gramma opens her eyes. She sits back in her chair. She slides her hand up from her chest to her throat. "I should know to stay away from grease."

Outside, a horn honks. Twice. And again.

"There's your mother," Gramma says.

Honk.

"Get going."

Honk, honk.

Gramma's breaths are coming easier. Her hands aren't shaking anymore. But her lips are still white.

"No. I can miss drama class today, Gramma."

"I'll let you know when I need you to baby-sit me," Gramma says. She takes another pill off my palm, holds it up to me, slips it under her tongue, and waves.

After grabbing my shoes from under the bed and my raincoat from the hall closet downstairs, I walk out onto the driveway.

Mom is waiting with the car running. The passenger door is open. Rain is dripping down on the front seat.

"Gramma had one of her spells, Mom."

"When?"

"Just now. She said it was from the chicken she ate."

"That's ridiculous. Where is she?"

"In her room."

Mom looks toward the attic window and frowns. She unbuckles her seat belt and swings her legs to the side.

53

She pulls her coat up over her head and runs into the house.

Rain hits the hood of the car. I watch out the smeared front window, but of course, I can't see what's going on in the attic. The motor hums.

It takes Mom nine minutes to come back to the car.

"I don't know, Bobbie. She says she's fine." Mom hesitates. Then she grinds the key in the ignition—the engine was already on—and shifts into reverse. She turns partway around and backs out of the driveway.

Swish, swish. The windshield wipers sweep the front window, and the line of cars easing along the highway blur, then come into view, blur, then come into view.

"Lights," Mom says to herself. "Four forty-five, we can still make it." Then to me she says, "You have improvisations today, right?"

"Huh?"

"Improvisations?"

"Yeah."

Mom veers onto the frontage road, turns left and left again into the parking lot of Hopkins Community Center, where my drama class meets.

While she parks the car, I dig in my pocket for a quarter. The phone is right in the foyer. Four rings. "Answer."

"Hello, Callahans."

It's Gramma. I hang up.

"Up here, dear," the drama teacher calls when I reach the auditorium.

The kids are assembled onstage. I climb up the steps and stand beside the dark-haired boy.

Our drama teacher's name is Sasha, and that's what we've been instructed to call her, not Miss or Ms. or Mrs. anything. One thing I like about her is that when she has us stand in lines, she doesn't make them be straight. She also doesn't make us do things if we don't feel comfortable doing them. Singing is one thing I don't do. When I'm a famous actress, I'm sorry I can't do musicals. There are other things I like about her, too. She's messy-looking, in a way that's nice. Her hair is all different lengths and sticks out all over the place. Her outfits never match. She wears big, floppy hats and jewelry made out of noodles.

"Rain!" Sasha suddenly shouts. "High and small: rain," she beeps out. *"Rain-ing, rain-ing,"* she booms.

> "The storm came up so very quick
> It couldn't have been quicker.
> I should have brought my hat along,
> I should have brought my slicker.
>
> "My hair is wet, my feet are wet,
> I couldn't be much wetter.
> I fell into a river once
> But this is even better."

Sasha collapses on a folding chair and laughs. "Mar-chette Chute," she says, holding up the ends of her wet hair. "Get comfortable, class, and get ready. We are going to be fruit."

The dark-haired boy takes off his shoes and wiggles his toes. He smiles shyly at me. I sit on the stage with my legs tucked under me and wave to my mom in the audience.

"Bobbie, would you mind being a pomegranate?" Sasha asks.

I close my eyes and think about the produce section in Super Value. I squat down, bunch up my arms, blow up my cheeks, hold my breath.

"Wonderful!" Sasha shouts. "Can everyone see it? Bobbie is getting rounder and redder. She is *becoming* a pomegranate."

At the end of class Sasha announces that the next time we meet we will concentrate on raw emotions. She assigns everyone an emotion to practice during the week. I'm assigned hopelessness. "And remember, class," Sasha says, standing on top of the folding chair, "art expresses what is within, but if there is nothing within, there is nothing to express. So, think. Think!"

CHAPTER 6

By dinnertime it has stopped raining. But dirty-looking clouds are heaped one on top of the other straight across the sky. This means it may storm again. I hope so. I want to use my umbrella. I'm on my way to Karen James's house, to help her with her homework. *"See you later,"* I yell, standing on the front stoop.

Dad opens the door. "If it starts lightning again, don't stand under a tree."

"I won't."

"Are you sure you don't want a ride?"

"No, thanks, Dad. Bye."

"Bye, sweetie."

Everything out here is soaked. Water is dripping from the trees. Puddles are all over the road. "Hello, worm."

Karen's neighborhood is up the hill from mine. After the hill you turn left and go through these white gates that no one ever paints, and there it is. I used to tell Karen that I could cut through her neighborhood mornings so we can walk to school together. Karen always had some reason why this wouldn't work. Last Tuesday, sitting in her kitchen, I asked if she wanted to walk with me tomorrow, and her mom jumped in. "I'm sorry, Bobbie, I drive Karen to school."

Karen peeled plastic off the seat of her chair and didn't look at me while her mom was talking.

"I know it's far-fetched," Mrs. James explained, "but I don't want Karen's dad to pick her up."

"That won't happen," Karen told her mom, "but I wish it would. Then I could ask him to come back home."

Whoosh. A car speeds by. Overhead a *V* of geese stretches across the sky. The wind blows and the trees' branches wave and I wave back, and the leaves softly slap one another.

At the top of the hill I turn left and hold on to the rough white gate. From this point to Karen's house I usually walk with my eyes shut, allowing myself a few peeks. Sasha says good actors and actresses are perceptive and we should work on developing *all* our senses. Tonight I don't have a whole lot of time, so I keep my eyes open and walk as fast as I can.

Down a hill, *squish, squish* (my tennies have water in the insides), veering right for the first bend in the road, skipping past Ropey (he's a dog), until I reach the culvert, where I take off my shoes and socks and wade through the water. Barefoot, I walk through the soggy grass and up the second hill and back around the circle.

When I'm almost to Karen's house, I pop open my umbrella.

"Bobbie!" Mrs. James says, flinging open the door. "Come in. Come in. Gosh, look at you. Your pants are soaked. I love the shoes. Did you wear them or just hold them all the way?"

"They leak."

"Dear. Well, we'll set them over the heat vent. I'll take the umbrella. Karen is in her room."

I walk down the hall to Karen's room. Everything seems upside down in this house. All the bedrooms are on the main floor, and the kitchen, living room, and dining room are upstairs. And it's quiet all the time, which has nothing to do with the upside-down part, other than it's different from what I'm used to. Sometimes it bothers me. The quiet is loud, and I want to go home and hear noise. Only Karen and her mom live here. They don't have any pets. Her dad left last year and took her brother with him.

"Hi, Karen."

"Hi."

"You working on math?"

"Trying."

Karen's books are spread over the floor. Paper and crunched paper and eraser shavings and little pointy pencils are all over the place. Each time I come it's this way. Karen spends hours every night doing homework. Around school people get known for things. Karen is known for being at the bottom.

"Numbers aren't real," Karen says to me. "I don't

understand things that aren't real. I try to pretend they are real, but then I get mixed up switching things around."

I plop down on the floor and pick up the piece of paper that she is bent over.

Karen sits and twists the ends of her hair and studies them. She shakes her head and keeps looking at her hair and says, "I get to the second step you're supposed to do, and then I forget what I'm supposed to do. So then I go back, and I can't remember figuring the first step. I don't know . . . maybe I should be in a school for dumb kids."

Somewhere I read that your brain is the size of a grapefruit and weighs as much as a head of cabbage. Once I heard Gramma say to Mom, "Who knows, maybe Karen James was dropped on her head in the delivery room." And as I'm thinking this, I say, "No, Karen," about being dumb, and the special school, and I'm wishing I could say something that would make her feel smart and important. Still, I'm wondering about those first two things and imagining a bruise somewhere on the inside of Karen's head.

In my bedroom I lie in the dark, looking from my bed out my window at the thin piece of moon hanging in the sky. The loud horn of the train blasts, and I count to ten. Then there is the sound of a huge chain dragging along the tracks as the train crosses the field on the side of our house.

I'm not sleeping on any pillow tonight. I want the best blood flow possible. Big thoughts, that's what I'm concentrating on. Famous people are said to have had profound matters on their mind as children. Profound matters don't seem to come to my mind naturally. So I am t-h-i-n-k-i-n-g.

Sister talked about deep time one day, a time so long and vast that no one can understand it. That's a big one. The earth is close to five billion years old, she said. A billion! And three and one-half million years ago a family in Africa left their footprints in a mud puddle.

I turn on my bedside lamp, kick my legs out and over my bed, and run to my desk. On the pad I write, "I am twelve years old and have forgotten most of my life." Then I switch the light off and go back to bed.

But I can't sleep. So I turn on my light again and stuff socks under my door. I don't want anyone to see my light on and know I'm up. From the bottom of my garment bag I pull out my sketchbook wrapped in two pairs of tights. My drawings are private. I hide them.

Once I did show Mom a few of them. "They're very different, Bobbie," she said. "What are they supposed to be?"

On a clean page inside my sketchbook I draw a house. (Don't you love new pages? I do.) The roof on this house points into the dirt. The bottom floor—I'm making it now—cuts across the sky. The lines on my house are pretty straight, even though I didn't use a ruler. I don't believe in rulers. I'm not too picky that way. Inside the house I draw a square. Inside the square I draw a girl. This girl is standing upside down and has a grapefruit for a head. Next, I plan to make a mother with a regular head.

"Bobbie!" Dad says, opening the door. "What are you still doing up?"

"Nothing."

"Nothing! What's all that stuff? And what are all these socks doing on the floor? Put it all away, and get into bed."

"*Okay*. You don't have to yell."

"I'm not yelling. Come on, I want to see you in bed."

Shoving my sketchbook under my bathrobe, I get up and crawl over the end of my mattress. Dad folds my covers under my chin. "You are something else," he says.

"Dad?"

"What?"

"Do you think Karen James's dad will ever come back?"

"Why do you always wait until you're supposed to be sleeping to ask me these kinds of questions?"

"I don't know. Do you?"

"Honey, how should I know?"

"That's not very good, Dad."

"Bobbie, I'm tired. Can't we talk about this tomorrow?"

After Dad is gone and the light in the hall disappears, I listen for the sound of water running through the walls. When it stops, I whisper the Gettysburg Address. (Sister made us memorize it.) The furnace kicks. The clock chimes. The house is silent. I ease out of bed and find my flashlight. I get out my pencil sharpener. Inside the closet I hang the flashlight from a belt and click it on: my spotlight. I open my sketchbook and start to draw.

First, the mother. I take my time and draw her well. I give her curly hair and earrings and a long neck. Then I draw a square around her. It's much bigger than the square I drew around the girl. There's room for a father inside. He went away, but he's coming back home. Nobody knows when.

CHAPTER 7

Dear Charlotte,

The All Saints Day party at church is coming up,
and same as last year, they're selling candy for a
nickel. I can't wait. I'm bringing ten dollars and
stocking up.

Karen James and I have been working hard on
our costumes. I'm going to be Joan of Arc. Karen
is going to be Blessed Isabelle of France. It hasn't
been easy making my costume, Charlotte. I'm
wearing a suit of armor, and I'm trying to be
authentic and make it out of real metal.

"Bobbie, eggs are ready. Gramma said to tell you to
come down *right* this minute. Or else."
"Or else what, Elissa?"
"*O-r-r Else.*"

Charlotte, when I grow up I am going to have
a doughnut shop next to my bedroom and eat

different kinds of doughnuts every morning for breakfast. I am never going to eat eggs. I am never going to make my kids eat eggs. Right now Gramma is calling me. I have to go eat eggs. Good-bye.

> Your best friend in the whole world,
> Bobbie

P.S. In English we are learning about outlines.

SKIPPING SCHOOL, WISHING I COULD:
    A. Read all day in a tree fort that comes with a refrigerator and a butler
    B. Steal a camel from the zoo and ride him
    C. Be discovered by a talent scout
    D. See you, Charlotte

"Here, Elissa, lick the envelope for me."

Elissa walks to my desk and holds out her tongue. I fold and crease my paper, slide it into the envelope, wipe the shiny strip on the flap across Elissa's tongue (I hate the taste of that), and pound, pound, to seal the letter shut.

Brown birds sit in a row on the telephone line. Behind them the sun looks as if it's bleeding over the sky. It's cold enough this morning for a sweater but too warm for a jacket. I'm wearing my navy cardigan sweater (what else?), my navy tights, and swiveling my hips as I walk because the legs of the tights are twisted. Elissa is wearing her new mittens and waving at cars.

"Knock, knock, Bobbie."

"I've heard it, Elissa."

"Knock, knock."

"All right, Elissa, who's there?"

"Banana."

"Banana who?"

"Knock, knock," Elissa says, and giggles.

"Who's there?"

"Banana."

"Banana who?"

Giggling. "Knock, knock."

"End it, Elissa. Who's there?"

"Orange," she says.

"O-r-a-n-g-e you glad I didn't say banana," I scream. Elissa stomps on my foot. Then she slugs me.

Traffic roars by on the other side of the chain-link fence that runs along Highway 12. The air smells of exhaust. Across County Road 101, in front of the gas station, a woman wearing a plastic hat and holding a shopping bag between her feet sits on the bus bench decorated with the picture of the smoking cowboy. Out the drive-up window of Burger Kingdom, a hand reaches out and delivers a paper cup to another hand.

"Hey, Elissa, let's tie one ankle together and walk the rest of the way to school."

"What for?"

"Just for something to do."

"No."

"Come on."

"No."

"Please."

"No."

"Are you still mad about that joke? You are. Here, look at my mouth." I run my finger across my closed lips. "Zip. Go ahead, Elissa. Tell me another joke."

"No."

"I *really* like those mittens."

No answer.

By the bank I stop in front of the mailbox, pull out my letter to Charlotte, and hand it to Elissa. Little kids love to mail letters. Elissa takes the letter and points her nose in the air. This means: big deal. *Cha-chung*, she closes the hatch of the mailbox and opens it again. The letter disappears. Elissa smiles and comes down off tiptoes.

At school Karen is waiting for me on the concrete steps outside the front door. "I lost my homework," she says.

"Aaah, too bad," a fifth-grade kid opening the door behind her jeers.

"I put it in my book, right in my book." Karen opens her math book, pages to the ground, and shakes it. "It's gone," she says. "I know I had it last night. I put it in my book. I know that. Then this morning I looked— Mom said to make sure I had everything—and it wasn't there. I put it there. I know I put it there."

"Go on into school, Elissa."

Elissa climbs the steps, reaches Karen, and pats her arm. After tugging on the door handle with both hands, Elissa slips into school.

"Mom said not to worry, that Sister would understand. Mom said she couldn't be late for work this morning. She can't afford to lose this job. She said Sister would understand." Karen blinks and blinks her eyes as she talks.

Kids file past her into school, and they stare. Some of them make rabbit ears behind her head.

"I'm afraid she won't understand," Karen says.

I walk up the steps and pull the sleeve of her sweater. "Come on, let's dump everything out and check again." I lead her around the corner of the building.

Karen watches me spill everything that's inside her backpack out onto the ground. English, science, religion, math—I flip through the pages of each book.

Squatting beside me, she says, "It was in my math book." She holds her knees and rocks back and forth.

I look in her folder and her spiral notebook and in stupid places like her pencil case.

"I don't want to get an incomplete and have points taken away," Karen says. "Sister has been giving me extra help—Mom can't afford the regular tutor anymore—and my grades . . . are . . ."

I wait and play with a stone on the ground, not saying anything because I hate when I can't talk and people talk for me.

"Still so bad," Karen says.

I shake off the straps of my backpack. From my back-pack I pull out my binder, open it, clip and unclip the metal rings. "Gimme your eraser," I say. With the clean edge of her smooth Pink Pearl I rub out "<u>Bobbie</u> Cal-lahan" from the top of my math homework. I blow off the eraser shavings and push my binder with the paper on top toward her. "Write your name."

Karen shakes her head.

"It's not as if we're cheating. Not exactly. I helped you with the homework. You *had* the right answers."

"I don't know," Karen says.

"Karen, the bell is going to ring."

"What about you?" she asks. "I can't let you get in trouble."

"One incomplete won't matter on my grade."

"Sister will get real mad."

"Sister is always mad at me. Look, it's up to you."

Only the toes of Sister's shoes show under her long skirt as she paces the buffed linoleum. Between rows she walks, looking intently at each one of us. "The more we take in, the better off we are," she says. First row, second row . . . "Our culture thrives on information. We attend lectures and workshops; we read books and articles; we listen to tapes; we watch television. Harold, stop fidgeting. The more we take in, the better off we are? Row three?"

Yes, the kids in the third row agree. They all nod their heads.

"Wrong!" Sister thunders.

The kids all switch their nods to noes—no, no, no!

"We have become closets of consumed and forgotten information," Sister says. "Dull, dark, musty-smelling closets. We blindly believe that the more we take in, the better off we are. Do we ever take time to sift through our closets?"

No one moves a head or opens a mouth: This could go either way.

"A question without an answer," Sister says, walking to her desk and sitting down. "It is your thought for the day."

Not my big thought. No way. My big thought has to be better than that. Besides, I like knowing a lot. I hate forgetting things, you know, like what year Balboa discovered the Pacific Ocean, why you turn your clock back, what I had for lunch last week. Lately I've been thinking about carrying Gramma's tape recorder around with me, so I can keep track of everything. Also, I've been considering memorizing a page of the dictionary each night, so when I grow up, I know a lot of big words.

"Most of our day will be devoted to testing," Sister says. "I hope you all remembered your two number two pencils."

That's right. All-day testing.

"I do regret the interruption in our normal class schedule," Sister tells us, "but it can't be helped. Because of the length of the test, we'll skip morning recess, break for lunch—"

70

"No recess!" a bunch of kids say.

"Gyp!"

"No fair."

"What is this?" Sister says. "Did I say you could voice your opinion? I was about to tell you that we will only have time for our last hour of class and that I will make up the lost recesses with a free hour when we're through with our week of testing."

It's hard to tell with Sister, but I think she's trying not to smile.

"Yes!" some of the kids holler. "A free hour!"

"All right!"

Ting, ting. Sister pushes the button of her bell. "I'm not finished yet."

What luck. I've been worrying this whole time for nothing. We're not even going to have math today. I can help Karen again tonight, and everything will be okay.

"The final hour of physical education will be dropped, however," Sister says, "in favor of mathematics."

I'm biting my pencil, making molar marks around the yellow edges, when Sister sounds the warning. For the past ten, maybe fifteen minutes I've been done with the test. Except for this one question. It's bugging me. What is the answer! Is it: All of the above? None of the above? "A" and "B" but not "C"? "B" and "C" but not "A"? "A" and "C" but not "B"?

"One minute," Sister announces. "One minute."

Ouch, my neck feels like it's going to fall off.

"Time is—"

Number four.

"—*up*. Pencils down. Close your booklets. Stand and stretch. Be seated."

Two o'clock.

Snap, snap. Sister clicks her fingers. "Pass your math homework to the front," she says. "Forward," she sings.

Desktops creak open. Heads disappear under the lids.

"Never fold your homework assignments," Sister says to no one in particular. "Keep them flat in a folder, nice and crisp and neat." She peels back the corners on the first row of papers. She nods her head in approval. Sorting through the second row's, she frowns and removes a paper, holding it away from herself. "Unacceptable, Mr. Brockton. I can barely read these numbers."

"But I can't write any better than that," Brian says.

" 'To live is to change,' " Sister says, " 'and to be perfect is to have changed often.' John Henry Newman. Do it over."

"Roberta Jean," Sister says when she gets to my row, "where is your homework assignment?"

"I don't have it, Sister."

"I can see that. Why not?"

Karen's hand slowly goes up.

"Not now, Karen," Sister says. "Well, Roberta, we're waiting."

"I just don't have it, Sister."

"Am I to understand that you simply—Karen, do you need to use the rest room?"

72

"No, Sister."

"Then please put your hand down. Simply did not do your math homework, Roberta?"

"No, Sister, I did it, but I don't have it."

Sister heaves her chest, and a long, loud breath comes out. "I presume you forgot your math homework at home, Roberta Jean. Just as you forgot your permission slip for the field trip last week, and your lunch money, and your overdue library books. Roberta Jean, you have to learn what it means to be responsible. I will not give you an incomplete mark on your grade. No, you will stay after school today and do last night's homework, plus twenty-five extra problems."

No, I won't. I'm sick of staying after school. "I didn't leave my paper at home, Sister. I lost it on the way to school. You see, I was reading it over this morning, you know, checking the answers over for a second time, when the wind came up and blew it right out of my hand." I hold up my hand and open my fingers so she can see how the wind took it. "I chased it for blocks, Sister, before it landed on the back of a semi. At that point I thought it best not to risk my life and run down the highway after it."

Tuh. Steven Walker sends a spitball into my hair. "Fat lie, Callahan," he whispers.

"Sit back in your seat, Mr. Walker," Sister orders. "Class," she says, "is there any wind today?"

"No-ooo," they answer.

"No wind. Roberta Jean, come to my desk. The rest of

73

you open your books to page fifty-eight and get busy."

I walk to her desk, making sure I don't look to the side at Karen on the way there. But I can feel her looking at me. And I want to say to her, "Happy? This is all your fault. If you hadn't have been so dumb in the first place, this wouldn't have happened." Then I feel bad for thinking this.

Directly in front of Sister, I stop. I doubt anyone is looking at page 58 in the math book. They're all looking at me. If I were one of them, I'd be looking at me.

"Roberta Jean," Sister says, folding her hands, "I don't like lying."

The floor is shiny. My shoes are untied.

"Look at me when I'm speaking to you, Roberta."

Sister's eyes are dull gray. Her hair is gray, too. And it's short and curly and never in her face. Wire spectacles sit on her nose; they don't move. Her skin is as pale as canned pears.

"Tonight, Roberta, you will write an essay entitled 'Truth.' Tomorrow you will present it to the class. Is that clear?"

"Yes."

"Good," she says, and puts a hand up her sleeve. She struggles; her fingers make tiny hills. Finally the handkerchief is out, and she blows her nose. "Tomorrow, Roberta Jean. No excuses."

CHAPTER 8

For dinner Gramma thinks big. Tonight we're having ribs, sweet potatoes, little red potatoes, green salad, fruit salad, cooked carrots, corn, and rolls.

We just finished saying grace. Mom is sitting at the head of the table, dishing up plates. Gramma is sitting at the opposite end of the table, closest to the kitchen, so, as Dad says, she can fly up and wait on us.

The phone rings, and Dad hollers, "We're eating! Don't answer it!"

"Butter, please," Elissa says.

"Do not start eating before everyone has a plate," Dad tells Elissa.

"Honey," Mom tells her, "not so much salt."

"Elissa Ann," Dad says, "did you hear your mother? Bobbie?"

"What?"

"I understand you had to stay after school again this afternoon."

I take my plate from Mom and start eating so I don't have to answer him right away.

"Bobbie," he says.

"Sister thinks I lied."

"What do you mean, Sister thinks?"

"I mean that I lied and Sister found out."

"Oh, for crying out loud."

"You lied to your teacher?" Mom says.

I look at Gramma. She's the only one I've told about giving Karen my math paper.

"What, it's a secret?" Dad shouts.

"Charles," Mom says, touching his hand, "keep your voice down."

"No, Lynne. No. We've tried your way, the let-her-work-it-out-on-her-own plan."

"Butter!"

Dad frowns at Elissa and passes her the butter. He gets up and goes to the refrigerator and takes out the ketchup.

"Why do you smear ketchup on everything?" Gramma says.

"Being tardy is one thing," Dad says; "lying is another."

"This *is* very upsetting, Bobbie," Mom says. "We've never known you to lie."

"Do you know," Dad says, "I got a phone call from your teacher twice this month at the office, saying that you flagrantly disobey rules? . . . Don't roll your eyes that way."

"Dad, Sister has so many rules it isn't even funny."

"Do all the other kids have these problems?" he asks.

"It sounds to me as if you're the only one having trouble following the rules."

"Bobbie," Mom says, "Sister is genuinely concerned about you. She says you have many talents, that you're well liked; she wants to help you."

"Teachers say that kind of stuff to parents, Mom. You don't know. You're not with her all day long."

Mom puts her hand to her mouth and shrieks.

Looped over the throw rug in front of the sink is Desdemona.

"It's a snake!" Mom screams. She runs to the back hall and slips on her shoes. "I hate snakes. Get it out of here."

"How did that get in here?" Dad says. He reaches over to the counter and picks up an empty saucepan.

"No! Ick!" Mom says. "Not with my good saucepan."

Before Elissa says anything, I look at her and mouth *dollar*, so she knows she has to give the one I gave her back if she tattles.

Gramma is laughing into her napkin.

Dad is still holding the pan. His mouth is partway open. "Did you do this, Mother?" he asks Gramma. "Is this some kind of joke?"

Gramma takes her napkin away from her mouth and says, "A donkey isn't a mule," and laughs harder. This is what Gramma always says when she doesn't want to get involved in an argument.

"Who cares about that now, Charles?" Mom says. "Get it out of this house before it crawls over here."

"Dad," I yell, "don't poke her!"

He's trying to slip a knife under Desdemona and lift her onto a newspaper.

"Dad, she's mine. I'll get her."

"What do you mean, she's yours?"

"She's my pet. I found her in the street. She's been in the aquarium. I had a screen over it. I don't know how she got out. But it won't happen again. I promise. I'll make sure she doesn't get out."

"No," Dad says. "We have an overgrown dog, fish, a turtle. We are *not* having a snake."

"But, Dad—"

"No buts."

"Alfred died, Dad," Elissa says.

"What? Talk to me later, Elissa," he says. "Alfred? I don't know any Alfred."

Elissa looks down at her plate. Alfred was her turtle.

Dad hands me the newspaper and motions with his head. "Take it outside."

I set the newspaper down. What do I need newspaper for? With one hand near her head, and the other near her tail, I pick her up and carry her outside.

You can always smell winter before it's here. I smell it now: part like our freezer, part like toast. I step off the stoop and walk out into the yard.

My parents wouldn't know if I sneaked around to the sliding glass door in the basement and took Desdemona back to my room. I could tape the screen to the sides of the aquarium. Then Desdemona wouldn't escape.

78

On the left side of the house, the side where my bedroom is, there are a bunch of pine trees. These trees are as tall as our chimney, and really fat. You can sit in the middle of them and hide from the rest of the yard. This is where I take Desdemona.

The sun is down, but there is still color in the sky. Looking up through the tops of the trees, I see pink clouds with orange edges. The wind is blowing. I'm sitting cross-legged on the ground, surrounded by pines. The wind is blowing, and the needles are saying, "*Sh-sh.*"

Desdemona is on my lap. Her tongue is flicking back and forth. Her body feels like cold patent leather shoes. I set her on the ground. She twists into S shapes and slides away.

CHAPTER 9

"Good thoughts," Gramma told me last night after I let Desdemona go. "Think good thoughts about Sister Alice. Bad thoughts make you ugly."

I know Gramma was talking about ugly insides. Even so, after she left my room, I pulled my eyes down with my fingers. Then I lifted my nose with my thumb and pushed it back against my face. I spread my lips and stuck out my tongue. After that I sat at my desk and wrote my essay.

It's fourth hour, English, and Sister is pulling down the window shades. The lights are off in our classroom. The overhead projector is set up in the back. The movie screen is set up in the front. We are getting ready to view split infinitives. Wow.

"No monkey business," Sister tells us. She turns on the overhead projector. A beam of light shoots across the room. Dust swirls inside the beam, and the projector makes a soft humming noise.

Sister is very neat. But I don't care too much about that. So I'm not sure if it counts as a good thought. She's smart. I like that. She gives Karen extra help. I like that, too. What else?

I rest my head on my arm, stretched out across my desk, and think.

The banks of fluorescent lights click on.

I lift my head. But not in time.

Sister makes a tepee with her hands in the direction of the door.

Other kids probably had their heads down, too; they just have better reflexes.

In the hall I slide my back against the slippery wall and sit on the floor. My knees are mountains. There is no operation that takes out part of your legs and sews them back together shorter. It's depressing.

Mr. George is down the hall bent under the water fountain. He waits a few moments after Sister leaves before he comes down the hall, swinging a wrench. His blue work shirt is wet under the arms. The veins on his forehead are showing.

"Katharine Hepburn," he says, crouching down next to me, "Katharine, Katharine, Katharine. I'm going to have to haul a desk up from the basement so you have somewhere to sit out here. Whatja do this time?"

"I was trying to do something nice, Mr. George." I mumble about good thoughts.

"Say what?"

"Sister caught me with my head down on the desk."

"Sugar, you've got to get your head down out of those clouds and aim it at that blackboard." He sets his wrench on the floor and takes two sticks of green spearmint gum out of his top pocket and hands one to

81

me. He rolls his piece up until it's the size of a peanut. Then he throws it to the ceiling almost and catches it with his mouth.

"I'm having a bad year, Mr. George."

"I can see that."

"Worse than bad."

"Some years are like that. Sixty-eight, sixty-nine, seventy"—*rwhooo*, he whistles—"those were bad years for me." He chews his gum. He pulls two more sticks out of his pocket and folds them into his mouth. "These things have a way of working themselves out, though. When I was young and in trouble, I said to myself, Clarence, you are better than they all think. I was. I knew it. And that's something I knew, and they didn't."

The door opens.

Mr. George picks up his wrench and stands.

I swallow my gum.

"Good morning, Sister."

"Good morning, Mr. George," she answers.

"I was just taking a little stretch here, Sister. I've been under that pipe all morning, and my back is killing me."

"I appreciate your intentions, Mr. George," Sister says, "but standing in the hall is supposed to be a punishment for Roberta."

Mr. George wiggles his wrench in front of my face and says, "Remember what I told you, kid." He winks at Sister and walks down the hall.

"You may come back into the room, Roberta," Sister tells me. "We're ready to hear you read your essay."

I go to my desk, lift the lid, and pull out my blue spiral notebook. "School stinks" and "Sister is a dictator" are written in code on the cover of the notebook.

Sister stands at the front of the room and signals me to come forward. She steps away from the spot where I'm supposed to stand.

I walk.

Everyone is looking at me.

"Pick up your feet," she tells me.

Everyone looks down at my feet.

At the front of the room I turn around and see the sign Steven Walker is waving: YOUR BRACES ARE UGLY!

But it doesn't matter. Walker is saying this to Bobbie Callahan. She's not here right now. Winston Churchill is giving this speech. He doesn't wear braces.

"Truth. Let's, for a moment, take a good look at truth. Truth is not merely the absence of falsehood, but more important it's the strength of one's convictions." On the word *conviction* I jab my fist in the air. (Last night I pounded on the sink, pretending it was a podium, but what the heck. You have to be able to improvise.) "The courage to be yourself." I throw up my arms. "To stand alone." I turn away from my class and face the blackboard.

"Of all the ridiculous things," Sister mutters.

At this point I'd planned to twirl around and face the front again, but—*scritch*—when I hear Sister's chair slide back from her desk and the clap of her shoes against the floor, I decide no, best not to.

83

Reaching over my left arm, Sister yanks my notebook away.

The class snickers.

"Be quiet!" she tells them.

The room is silent. I know without looking that Sister is reading my essay. I hear a page turn. Now a second page. I glance upward at the clock above the blackboard. Fifteen minutes until lunch. What am I supposed to do? Just stand here?

"Do us a favor, Roberta, and face the front."

Everyone starts laughing again.

This time Sister doesn't seem to notice. She keeps reading.

Against my chin I crack all the knuckles in my fingers. Then I shuffle my feet, pretending I'm interested in something on the floor. How long does it take to read an essay? I look out the window. Though really, out of the corner of my eye, I'm watching the kids laugh. Steven Walker is howling, and Sister isn't saying a thing to him. Katherine Anderson is actually giggling. Sam is even laughing. Forget I ever liked him. Everyone is laughing. Everyone except for Karen James. Karen just looks scared.

Suddenly I'm smiling, going along with the rest of them, passing it off as a joke. I don't know why, because inside, it doesn't feel funny.

"This amuses you?" Sister says to me. She holds my notebook up to the class and says, "Without all the theatrics this paper is very satisfactory. You could all learn something from this essay. Good work, Roberta."

Dear Charlotte,

I have great news. I'm a playwright. Sasha (that's my drama teacher) asked for a volunteer to write the script for our Christmas play *Snow White and the Seven Dwarfs* and—*ta-da!*—she picked me. Can you believe it?

We're putting on the play for schools and a couple of nursing homes and one night for anyone who wants to come. Sasha says we need to start preparing. So we're going to take our time demonstrating our emotions and spend most of the class hour painting scenery, and making papier-mâché heads for the dwarfs, and stuff like that.

So far Sasha hasn't called on me to demonstrate my emotion, and I'm glad. I've been so busy lately that I haven't had a chance to practice being hopeless. I plan on doing it soon.

Besides writing the play, I have an acting part, but it's small. I'm Snow White's father. I wish I could be Snow White and write the script, but I guess you can't have everything. Leslie Cummings is Snow White. She has very little feet.

I found out two important things this week. The first thing is that Sister doesn't spy on me. The reason she rides her bike through my neighborhood is that she tutors Karen. Don't tell anyone. I think Karen is embarrassed about being tutored. I know I can trust you, Charlotte.

The second thing I found out is that the *B* on Sam's notebook stands for Beverly. Liking someone and then not having them like you back is a very hard thing.

That's all. I'm writing this letter outside, and I'm sick of holding the paper down. I'm mailing you a survey. It's the simple, modern way to tell me all about yourself. Send it back as soon as you can.

I always think of you.

    Bobbie

CHAPTER 10

It's five minutes after nine, and I'm already at the pond. I didn't waste any time getting here. After church I went straight from the car to my bedroom and changed into my jeans. I didn't read the funny papers or eat pancakes. "I've got work to do," I told everyone. And it's true, I have. I'm here at the pond feeding a goose. This is only the beginning.

The goose is all alone. His mate got run over by a car, and now he won't leave the pond. He didn't fly away with the rest of the geese when the weather turned cold.

"Here you go." I toss him the last bit of bread. He shakes his head while he eats it. He sniffs the air. Then he sniffs the ground. The grass is white and crisp. Last night we had our first frost. "Good-bye, Goosie."

I brush the crumbs off my pants and walk up the hill. The goose follows me. Dad says if I keep feeding this goose, he'll forget about his mate and want to hitch up with me.

Along the shoulder of McGinty Road I pedal my bike no-hands. Then I grab the handlebars and hold my feet above the pedals. "*Ahhh!*" I yell at the telephone poles.

Crows fly off the crossbars. I'm having fun, messing around before I work on my assigned emotion for drama class. Today is my day to study hopelessness.

The problem is I've never felt hopeless. But I figure Raymond, the homeless guy, has. I figure he pretty much feels hopeless all the time. So I'm going to find him and follow him around.

The colored doors of the shops along Lake Street are locked. The sidewalks are empty. Nobody is around this early on a Sunday. "Yip-pee!" I ride past the popcorn trolley, the black lamp posts, the skinny, bare trees. Across the street is the lake, wrinkly and full of the sun. I ride by the rock shop and the bookstore, pull up hard on my handlebars, pop a wheelie, come down over the curb, and race like crazy to the post office. I like to pretend people are chasing me. By the time I reach the blue mailboxes, I'm out of breath.

So far I haven't seen Raymond. But I know he's here someplace. He always is.

I've made a list of stores where I've seen Raymond hanging around, and I'm on my way (the long way) to number one: the deli department in the grocery store. The deli department has tables you can sit at without buying anything. There's also free coffee.

At first, when Raymond showed up, there was a lot of talk in our town. Who is this guy? Our neighbor, Mrs. Whitepost, even called the cops. She said she was worried about him. She said she was worried about the children in our town, too.

"Like you, dear," she said one day while I was drinking lemonade on her porch and petting her dog. "You know me," she said, "I'm very direct." (Gramma calls her a busybody.) "They told me he was harmless," Mrs. Whitepost said. "There's nothing wrong with him. Other than he doesn't have a home or a job."

In the parking lot of the grocery store a boy is selling pumpkins. I slant my bike against the brick planter and go inside. (That's the good thing about riding a crummy bike. No one wants to steal it.)

Nope. No Raymond. The tables in the deli department are empty.

On my way out of the store, I stop at the suggestion box. I write on a piece of paper: "Not all your customers like coffee. How about serving free pop?"

The next stop on my list is the drugstore. Raymond likes to rock back and forth on his feet in front of the drugstore. As it turns out though, I don't have to look there. I already see him. Raymond is in the bus stop shelter.

I cross the intersection and ride down a ways to get there. I don't go inside the shelter. That would be too obvious. I flick the kickstand down on my bike and sit on the bench that's right outside the shelter. I have a great sideview of Raymond.

In downtown Minneapolis there are other men Mom says are homeless. One guy on Nicollet Avenue shouts from the rim of a fountain. This guy would be a lot more fun to watch than Raymond. Raymond isn't doing anything except sitting and smoking. He's not even blowing rings. If I smoked, and I wouldn't, I'd blow rings.

Doesn't move a whole lot. Remember this, I say to myself. This might be part of hopelessness. Sits at a bus stop but doesn't get on the bus. (It pulled up a second ago.) Remember this, too.

All of a sudden Raymond turns his head and looks through the glass at me. I look away. He comes out of the shelter and drops his cigarette on the ground in front of me and smashes it with his shoe. He's not looking at me anymore. He just looked at me for a second. But it gave me a weird feeling.

I'm going to sit here awhile before I get up and follow him. He's about fifty feet away from me now. I'll just sit here awhile, and when he gets as far as the cleaner's, I'll get up and start walking my bike after him.

Raymond is wearing brown pants that look as if they once belonged to a suit, an army jacket, an orange hunting hat, and beat-up running shoes. He's not wearing anything on his hands. His hands are in his pocket.

He just passed the cleaner's. I take off my mittens and stuff them in the pocket of my jacket, get off the bench, and grab my bike. I don't want him to get too far ahead of me.

"Don't just imitate what you want to be. Become it," Sasha says.

I'm walking beside my bike, without any mittens. I hear the traffic. I feel my feet. I'm going somewhere, but I don't know where. I'm Raymond.

90

Raymond crosses Broadway and passes through the school gate. He goes by the monkey bars and the basketball court. He goes by the whirl-go-round. He goes by the slide. He walks past Father's driveway and climbs the steps of the convent.

I'm staying here on the corner of Broadway. I'm sitting on my bike seat, with my toes touching the ground. I'm leaning low over my handlebars and watching. What the heck is Raymond doing?

The convent is a two-story brick building, same as school. Mom said that when she was young, the place was full of nuns. But now there are only Sister Alice and Sister Mary.

Sister Alice is opening the door and talking to Raymond. Maybe Raymond is asking Sister for money. Maybe because she's a nun, he thinks she's nice. Maybe she is telling Raymond to get a job. That's what she would say to me if I were him. Which right now I am.

He's going inside. This is something. I didn't think people actually let Raymond inside their houses.

Pushing off my feet, I ride over the curb and go around to the back entrance of the school parking lot. By the outside stairs leading down to the cafeteria, I park my bike. I run across Father's side yard, then his backyard, all the way around his house to the corner of the garage. I wait at the garage and listen to my heart socking me in the chest.

It's all right, I tell myself. This is for a class. I leave the corner and sneak up to Sister's front door. There's a window on the door, so I keep off to one side. With my back against the brick, I take a look. (I've seen this done on TV hundreds of times. I've practiced it at home, too.) They're not in the back hall. Crouching low, I creep across the front stoop, hop over the iron railing, step over Sister's evergreens, and peer inside the bay window. The bay window looks into the dining room, and from the dining room you can see into the living room. They're not in either of these rooms. The only other windows on the bottom floor are the kitchen windows. I bet you anything they're in the kitchen.

"Roberta!"

Sister Alice is standing on the front stoop, holding the door open with her foot.

I didn't hear the door open. I didn't hear anything. Nothing.

"Get over here!" Sister says.

I could run for it, but it's not worth it. I'd have to face Sister on Monday. I walk over to the bottom of the steps. "I was working on an assignment for my drama class, Sister. I wasn't trying to look at you."

"Get inside. I'm not heating the outdoors."

I climb the steps and go in.

"So, you were assigned to hide under my windows."

"No."

"Interesting—isn't it, Roberta?—that Mr. Ohms told me some kid followed him here. Are you that kid? Is this your idea of a joke?"

"No."

"What then?"

"I was suppose to work on being hopeless. I thought that—"

"Don't follow people, Roberta."

I nod and turn to leave. Sister went easy on me. Probably because it's the weekend. From time to time I bump into teachers in stores and restaurants, and I've noticed that most of them are nicer on the weekends.

"Put your things on the bench," Sister says, as if she can't see I'm ready to leave. "And come into the kitchen."

I unwind my scarf and take off my jacket and shoes. I feel very stupid. I'm going to quit being Raymond. It's hard enough being me.

In the kitchen Raymond is sitting at Sister's table in his stocking feet. The kitchen smells. It's a combination of people smell and scrambled eggs. Boy, I hate that smell. I want to put my hand over my mouth, but I stop myself.

A man and a woman are sitting on either side of Raymond. They both have shriveled, baggy skin, huge eyes under their glasses, and white hair. Their jackets say "Aqua Bowl."

"Mother, Dad," Sister says. "I'd like you to meet one of my students, Roberta Jean Callahan."

Her parents! I don't believe this. They're her parents. Sister Alice's parents.

The dad puts two fingers to his forehead and salutes me.

The mother says, "Hello, dear."

"Hi," I say to them. I try to sound enthusiastic.

"Mr. Ohms," Sister says, bending slightly toward him and resting her hand on the back of his chair, "Roberta didn't mean to bother you. She just wanted to meet you."

I know Raymond Ohms heard Sister because he looks up from his eggs. But he doesn't say anything.

I say, "Hi, Mr. Ohms." (I never knew his last name before Sister told me it.) I try to think of something else I can say besides "hi," so he doesn't think I was teasing him by following him here. But I can't think of anything.

"How do you like school, dear?" the mother asks me.

"Good," I lie.

Raymond eats his eggs. He scrapes his fork against his teeth with each bite. His top lip has some kind of sore on it.

"Have a seat, Roberta," Sister says. Her voice doesn't sound anything like the way it does at school. "Dad," she says, "eat up before everything gets cold. You, too, Mother."

"We're snowbirds," the mother says to me. "Tomorrow we leave for Arizona."

"And I'm all ready," the dad says, pretending to swing a golf club.

They both giggle.

"Can't she cook!" the dad says to me about Sister Alice, as if I'm supposed to know.

"Oh, come on, Dad," Sister says to him. She turns red, something I've never seen Sister Alice do before.

"Sit down, dear," the mother says to me. "The more the merrier."

"That's okay," I tell her.

"Go, ahead, Roberta," Sister says. "Make yourself at home. I'll pull a chair in from the dining room."

"Thanks, but I have to go." I back up toward the doorway to the dining room. "It was nice meeting all of you."

"Lovely meeting you, Roberta," the mother says. "Bye-bye."

"Have fun in Arizona," I tell them.

"Will do," the dad says.

"I'll be back in a minute," Sister says, and she follows me through the dining room and into the foyer. She stands and watches me while I put on my shoes. "Tie them, Roberta, so you don't trip."

I bend down again and tie my shoes. Then I pull on my jacket and wind my scarf around my neck. I take my mittens out of my pockets and put them on, wishing I knew how to disappear.

"No hat, Roberta?"

"No," I tell her. "I don't like hats all that much. Sorry about peeking in your windows, Sister." I say this trying to turn her doorknob, but it's slippery.

She reaches around me, twists the knob, and pulls open the door. She follows me outside.

95

The wind smacks us a good one the minute we step out. There was no wind before. But now it's coming in big gusts. Sister's hair blows up and back and falls down again behind her bobby pins. My hair blows all around and lands in my mouth. I pick it out. Am I supposed to say something else?

Sister stands holding herself against the cold. "I thought you should know, Roberta, that Karen James came to me and told me what the true story behind the math incident was."

The math incident, when I switched papers with Karen. It happened a week ago, and I thought it was over. I mean, I thought after my essay and everything that sister wasn't going to say anything more about it.

"I knew it was your work all along that Karen handed in. I do know my students' work, Roberta. But that's not what I want to tell you. I want to tell you that I think Karen needs to take her knocks at school like everyone else. She doesn't need people protecting her all the time."

"I know that." (I really don't know it, but I say it anyway.) "And I don't usually lie. Not about big things anyway. I'm better than you think." Why did I say this? It sounded dumb.

"What, Roberta?" Sister straightens up and puts her hands on her hips. "I've been teaching school for thirty-five years. *All* of my students have been good. Yes, I've had to dig it out of many. Turn them upside down and shake it out of them. But that's my job. Do not confuse irritation with goodness, Roberta. You are very good and very irritating. I have high hopes for you. Now go home so I can get back to my guests. And don't dilly-dally the way you usually do. It's supposed to snow this afternoon. And for goodness' sakes, Roberta, stand tall. Honestly, you're going to ruin your spine stooping all the time. Someday you'll appreciate your height. I was once the tallest girl in my class, too."

And this is supposed to make me feel better? Sister is tall now. She is about as big as my dad, who is over six feet. I *am* hopeless.

But then to tell you the truth, thinking back on everything Sister said, I'm feeling pretty good.

"So long, Sister."

"Good-bye, Roberta Jean."

It's ten after ten, and I'm supposed to be in bed. But I'm not. I'm in my closet, writing a letter. The letter is to Raymond Ohms. I'm going to send the letter to Sister and ask her to give it to Mr. Ohms. I could give the letter to him personally, but I'm afraid he wouldn't take it. There is a package that goes with the letter. That's part of it, too.

Dear Mr. Ohms,

I'm sorry I followed you. I didn't mean anything bad by it.

I'm sending you gloves. They're new. I hope you like them.

If someone follows you again, it won't be me.

Yours very truly,
Bobbie

P.S. I'm the girl in Sister's kitchen (Roberta).

CHAPTER 11

We left the smell of turkey cooking in the kitchen, and the Thanksgiving Day parade that was on TV, and the giant turkey you can color (and mail in and maybe win a prize) in the variety section of the newspaper. But I don't mind. Not really. I'm the one that asked to go with Gramma.

We're parked at the end of our road, kitty-corner from the bus stop. Mom and Gramma are in the front seat. I'm in the back.

"Sarah, let me give you a ride."

"Public transportation is fine for me," Gramma says to Mom.

Gramma wanted to drive Dad's car to the nursing home. But Dad said the freezing rain has made the roads too dangerous.

"Next time I'll take my own car."

"Sarah, you've never driven the convertible in the winter."

I scrunch my toes and jiggle my knees. The heater is on. But it's still cold.

"So how come you can drive on the roads?" Gramma asks Mom.

"Here it comes, you guys," I tell them. "The bus."

"What if you had a spell, Sarah?" Mom says it fast, and it comes out sounding as if she's been trying not to say it.

"My doctor didn't say I couldn't drive."

"You guys. The bus." I slide across the backseat, toward the door on Gramma's side.

"Sarah," Mom says, touching her shoulder. "Wait. I don't want you to leave on a bad note. I have a good idea. Why don't you stay home today? We'll eat at a reasonable hour for one Thanksgiving. We'll relax."

"That's your good idea?" Gramma says. "I'm going to the nursing home to visit Ima, same as every other Thanksgiving. I don't care what you do."

I get out of the car, open the front door, and hold my arm out for Gram. She picks her shopping bag off the floor, reaches for my arm, and rocks once to get herself out of the car.

"Now don't hurry," Mom says, coming around the front fender and taking Gramma's other arm.

We wait for a second—hooked together—while a car drives past. The car slides through the stop sign, turns, and fishtails onto the frontage road.

"Slow down!" Gramma hollers.

"Sarah," Mom says, "I didn't mean to say anything to hurt your feelings."

"Oh, pooh, Lynne," Gramma says. "Don't trip all over yourself apologizing the way you always do."

Mom breathes so everyone can hear and looks over Gramma's head at me.

Gramma takes tiny sliding steps. "And see that you watch my turkey. You have to baste it often so it doesn't dry out."

"I know how to cook a turkey," Mom says.

"Last year the turkey was too dry," Gramma says. "I could barely swallow it."

"Hello, ladies," the bus driver calls. "Cold enough for you?" He gets out of his seat, comes down a step, and holds out his hand to Gramma.

Gramma takes his hand, while Mom and I give her a push to get her on the first step. Gramma is very short, and it's hard for her to climb big steps. She pauses, steps up again, grabs the silver pole.

"Hang on to her today," Mom says, and pats me on the back. Then she calls, "Good-bye, Sarah."

Gramma doesn't answer. She's busy with her purse.

I climb the steps and wait while she pushes money into the machine. I don't offer to help because she'll get mad. Gramma has been getting mad easily lately. Really she only has to pay a quarter to ride the bus. But she refuses to get a senior citizens' pass.

I sit down beside her in the long seat behind the driver.

The bus driver pulls the door shut. We shake in our

seats a little as he starts down the road. We're going downtown. Then we transfer to another bus.

"Gramma, I wish you guys wouldn't fight so much."

Gramma sets her shopping bag between her legs. "I can't help it," she says. "I'm too old to have people telling me what to do." Then she tells me, "Always hold your purse in your lap when you ride the bus." She tugs on the handles to show me it's hard to rip off. "Tape some extra change in your shoe."

There are cardboard turkeys and Pilgrims and cornucopias decorating the walls in the lobby of the nursing home. An orange covered with cloves is hanging from the ceiling over the front desk.

"Hello, Sandy," Gramma says to the lady behind the desk.

Sandy is on the phone. She wiggles her fingers to say hello.

Ping. The elevator door opens. We go in and push "3." *Ping.* The door opens again, and we walk out in front of another desk.

"Mildred," Gramma says. "Happy Thanksgiving."

"Happy Thanksgiving, Sarah," Mildred answers.

(Mildred looks old enough to be a patient.) "You brought company."

"My granddaughter," Gramma says proudly.

"Isn't that nice," Mildred says. Mildred has glasses with sparkles in the frames, and designs painted on her fingernails. "Are you two eating with us today?"

102

"You bet," Gramma says.

"Wonderful," Mildred says. "We're having some special entertainment." She winks at me. "Glad you came today, hon."

"What's the entertainment?" I whisper to Gramma when we're away from the desk.

"I have no idea," Gramma says.

We walk down a hall to another hall. Every room looks pretty much the same. The TVs are near the ceiling. All the beds are made.

Mrs. Swanson is at the end of the second hall, sitting out in the hall, in a chair with a tray attached.

"Ima," Gramma says before we reach her.

Mrs. Swanson's eyes are open, but it looks as if she could be sleeping.

"Ima Rose," Gramma says, and bends down and kisses Mrs. Swanson on the cheek. "Happy Thanksgiving." She sets her shopping bag on the floor, opens her purse, takes out a handkerchief, and wipes off the lipstick that she left on Mrs. Swanson's face.

Mrs. Swanson straightens her head. She looks at Gramma and says, "Sarah?"

"Yes, I'm here. It's taken me awhile to get here. But I'm here. The weather is nasty, Ima. Cold and ugly."

"Mercy me," Mrs. Swanson says.

"Look, Ima. I brought my pal." Gramma puts her hand on my back. "You remember Bobbie. Charlie's girl?"

"Never saw her before in my life," Mrs. Swanson

says. She moves her head up and down, looking at my feet and then at my head and back again. "You're very tall."

"Yes," Gramma answers for me. "She's tall. She takes after Great-Grandpa Marshall. He was six-four. And of course, my Charlie is well over six feet."

"Charlie is a pipsqueak," Mrs. Swanson says.

"No, he's not," Gramma says. "Ask Bobbie."

"Who's Bobbie?"

"Bobbie," Gramma says, turning her thumb toward me. "Look at this head of hair, Ima." Gramma grabs a chunk of my hair and shakes it. "Is that not my hair? I've got more hair than anyone I know. My hairdresser tells me all the time, 'You've got more hair!' And you, Ima. You look wonderful. I love that dress."

Mrs. Swanson looks down at the front of herself. "What have I got on?"

She's wearing a red dress with a white collar, white over-the-knee hospital socks, and fluffy blue slippers. You can see each bump in her hair where someone took out a roller.

"You really look good, Ima," Gramma says. "Bobbie, go ask Mildred if it's all right to wheel Ima into the lounge. And get us some coffee. Ask Mildred. She'll tell you where it is."

I get to the end of the hall when a lady calls to me from her room. "You there!"

I step back and look in through the doorway. The

lady is sitting on the edge of her bed, and another lady, a nurse, I think, is helping her on with her sweater.

The nurse turns and smiles at me. "Hi."

"Hi," I say, and quickly walk away.

"You there!" I hear again.

I turn around. A man with a stethoscope around his neck just passed that same lady's room.

"Hi, Mrs. Lem-ky," the man says without stopping. He catches up to me. "Don't tell me," he says. "Your parents made you come and visit a relative today?"

"I don't have a relative here. I came with my gramma to see her friend."

"I'm Joe," he says (I knew that from his name tag), and puts out his hand.

I shake it. "Hi."

"Who's your gramma's friend?"

"Mrs. Swanson."

Joe smiles. "You're Sarah's grandkid. Bobbie. And you have a little sister named E—"

"Elissa," I tell him.

"Elissa," he says, snapping his fingers down toward his knee. "I knew it began with an *E*. Man, they broke the mold when they made your grandmother. How's she been feeling?"

"Good."

"That's good," Joe says. "She wasn't too hot the last time she was here."

We turn down the first hall that Gramma and I walked

down when we came off the elevator. Joe stops at the front desk and hands Mildred a white card.

"I'll be down to see your grandmother in a few minutes," he says to me, walking off.

"What's the matter, hon?" Mildred asks me.

"Nothing. I just need to know where the coffee is. My gramma asked me to get her some."

"Right down there, hon. There's a beverage cart on your left. You can't miss it."

Really, something is the matter. I feel as if Gramma told Joe a secret that she didn't tell me. I ask her every day how she feels, and she always says fine.

The beverage cart is a stainless steel shelf with wheels. I pick up an orange tray and set three cups on it. In two cups I pour coffee, and in the third cup I make instant cocoa. I think about not bringing Gramma her cream. Mom and Dad say it's bad for her heart. But then I think, no, I better. So I put one little packet on the tray.

"Need a hand carrying that?" Mildred asks as I walk by the front desk. Two ladies talking to her turn around and look at me.

"No, thanks," I tell her.

"Okay, hon."

Halfway back to Gramma and Mrs. Swanson, Joe comes by and says, "I had the aide wheel Mrs. S back to her room so I could get a set of vitals. I'll show you the way."

Joe leads me five doors down to number 322. "Look who I met in the hall, Sarah."

106

"Bobbie," Gramma says, "I was just going to come out and look for you."

"Wow! Mrs. S," Joe says. "You have a new dress on. Did your son send that? It's very pretty."

"Jamie is down at the creek. But I told him to be home by noon," Mrs. Swanson says.

"You're in your room at the nursing home, Mrs. S, visiting with Sarah. This is Joe. I'm your nurse for this afternoon."

"What's that?" Mrs. Swanson says.

"I said I'm your nurse. I'm going to be taking care of you this afternoon."

"Oh, no," Mrs. Swanson says.

"What do you mean 'oh, no.' Thanks a lot. Do you remember your name today?" Joe asks her.

"Of course I do. Ima Rose Swanson."

"That's right," Joe says. "And do you know what day it is?"

Mrs. Swanson opens her mouth but doesn't say anything.

"It's turkey day, Mrs. S. Thanksgiving."

Poof, poof, poof. Joe squeezes the black ball on the blood pressure cuff. *Fruuu.* He releases it.

"Am I alive?" Mrs. Swanson asks him.

When Joe leaves, Gramma reaches into her shopping bag and pulls out a hat. It's a red hat with black netting and a feather—the kind rich ladies in cartoons always wear. "Look, Ima," she says. Gramma gets up and starts to put the hat on Mrs. Swanson's head.

"No, don't!" Mrs. Swanson says, ducking down in her chair. "You'll crush the ABCs."

Gramma pulls the hat back.

"They've been in my head all morning, and they're all mixed up. The *B* is where the *J* should be. The *X* is on top of the *Z*." Mrs. Swanson lightly touches her hair. She makes a face. "I can't straighten them out. It's dreadful."

Gramma puts the hat back inside the bag. Then she picks up her purse and takes out a comb. She goes over to Mrs. Swanson, tilts her head forward, and makes little parts in her hair. She holds up a mirror.

"They're all in order," Gramma says.

Mrs. Swanson looks in the mirror. Then she looks at me.

I nod.

Lights are on in the city. We go and stop, but no one gets on the bus. The bus stops are empty. It's even colder out than it was this afternoon. Frost in the shape of ferns is on the windows. I scratch it away until my fingernails are full of little white shavings. Snow is twirling down outside.

"Look, Gram."

"Snow," Gramma says, leaning over me.

"Hey, Gram, was that woman who played the accordion a patient or whatever?"

"A resident?"

"Yeah. Was she?"

108

"I don't know, Bobbie."

"Do you think those were her real teeth?"

"Nobody's teeth are that white," Gramma says. "Except for mine." She grins at me. Her teeth are yellow.

"I didn't think so either. It's a sad place. Huh, Gram?"

"Yup," Gramma says.

The bus goes by the West Bank at the University of Minnesota. It goes by the old train depot, then downtown. We pass under garlands strung across the skywalks and giant red bells. We turn down Nicollet Avenue. A newspaper is blowing along the street, getting stuck on trash bins and benches.

Gramma puts her head against my shoulder and closes her eyes.

CHAPTER 12

"What is it?" Elissa asks me.

"You know what it is."

"Oatmeal. I hate oatmeal."

I take the wooden spoon and dish the oatmeal out of the pan and into two bowls. Then I open the cupboard and get out the raisins. On top of Elissa's oatmeal, I arrange the raisins to make a smiling face. "Your oatmeal likes *you*, Elissa." I slide the bowl across the counter.

Elissa catches the bowl and pushes it away. "I'm having Rice Krispies."

"No, you're not."

"Girls. What's the problem?" Mom walks into the kitchen, scrunching the ends of her wet hair.

"You told me to make breakfast, and I made oatmeal, and Elissa won't eat it."

"Elissa, eat what your sister fixed," Mom tells her.

"Bobbie is smiling," Elissa says. "Mom! She's teasing me."

"Stop it. The both of you. You girls are going to have to cooperate in this kitchen while Gramma is gone."

"I'm glad Gramma is gone," Elissa says. "She's been too crabby. Dad thinks so, too. He told Uncle Harry at the airport that 'Gramma has been as ornery an owl lately.' "

Mom picks up the oatmeal pan and carries it to the sink. "Gramma is having a hard time, Elissa."

"I'm having a hard time, too," Elissa says. "At school. Adam has been stealing my milk money."

"What do you mean?" Mom asks.

"He takes my quarters," Elissa says.

"Who's been taking your quarters?" Dad asks, walking into the kitchen.

"Adam," I tell him, while Elissa takes a bite of her oatmeal.

"How do you know it's him?" Mom says to Elissa.

"Did he tell you that?" Dad wants to know.

Mark this day down. December 2. There's a problem at school, and it doesn't have anything to do with me.

"People don't tell you when they're stealing from you," Elissa says. "But I know it's him. He's been drinking two milks at lunch."

"Gosh!" Mom says. "Look what time it is. We've got to get going. Elissa, you tell that kid to cut it out."

"And if he doesn't stop, tell your teacher," Dad says.

"Be sure to rinse your bowls when you're through eating, girls," Mom tells us. "And dress warm. You have to wear snowpants. It's cold out."

Roo-roo, roo-roo. I walk down the driveway, listening to the legs of my snowpants rub together. Elissa has a

111

heavier one-piece snowsuit, and hers makes a different sound. *Shoe shoe shoe shoe.*

Snow is everywhere. There isn't a place out here that doesn't have it. Snow has blown in wavy drifts across the yard. Snow is piled on roofs and mailboxes and trees. If Gramma were here, she'd tell us: "You two are lucky to have warm clothes on a day like today."

"We hate snowpants, Gramma."

"You two are lucky to even have legs!"

Gramma is always telling us things we're lucky to have—our legs and eyes and stuff like that.

Gramma took off all of a sudden to see Aunt Helen. It's weird because she hates to fly in airplanes. She hasn't flown in six years, not since Grandpa died. She's staying three days at Aunt Helen's. After that she's flying to Seattle to see her cousin. After that some other place to see her niece. After that she's coming home. I can't wait.

Elissa and I climb onto the huge mound along the road made by the snowplow. No cars—jump! We land in the street.

Puff. I blow a cloud of smoke in front of my face. "I got a letter from Charlotte yesterday, Elissa."

"Good," she says.

I stop walking and unzip my backpack. "Here, I want you to read it to me. I crossed out all the parts I don't want you to see."

Elissa takes the letter. "I can't read cursive." She hands it back to me.

112

"Okay, I'll read the parts I want to hear out loud. You repeat them. 'Dear Bobbie.' "

" 'Dear Bobbie.' "

"Make it sound better than that, Elissa. Come on. Project. Show some feeling. 'Dear! Bobbie!' "

" '*Dear* Bobbie.' "

"Forget it. I'll read it myself."

" 'Dear Bobbie,

" 'I'm sorry you haven't gotten any letters from me in a while. It's not that I haven't written you. I have. It's just that I never mailed the letters. Two were in my drawer, and one I lost on the way to the store. Mom got real mad when she found that out. She said I'd forget my head if it weren't attached. Bobbie is going to think you've forgotten her, she said. But you know I could never forget you.' "

"Did you hear that, Elissa?"

"Nice," Elissa says. She hikes her backpack higher on her shoulders.

" 'It's hard being the new kid. You get teased. The kids tell me I talk like my nose is plugged up. Two other kids in my class are new, too, but they're both boys. I've made three friends so far. I sit with them at lunch, and one rides my bus. I ride the bus for an hour. It's boring.

113

" 'My school is a lot bigger than Saint Francis. The only thing better about it is that we have lockers and you don't.

" 'I miss you. I miss the things we did. I told my mom and dad that if we moved back to Minnesota, I'd do anything. I'd share a room with my brother if I had to.

" 'Love,
Charlotte

" 'P.S. In your survey you asked, "Who is your best friend?" Then you named a bunch of people. Don't you know that you're my best friend?' "

"Mine, too, Charlotte. What do you say to that, Elissa?"

"Nice."

"Nice? Is that all?"

The snowplow is coming. I hear the clanking metal. In a second we see it, yellow lights flashing at the top of the hill. "Hurry, Elissa. Lay down on top of the mound so you can get buried when it goes by. I promise I'll dig you out."

"No."

"Okay, here." I grab the shoulder of her snowsuit and pull her with me over the mound, into Old Mr. Sims's yard, to wait while the snowplow passes.

Mr. Sims is snowblowing his driveway. He shuts the machine off when he sees us. "Hello, girls."

"Hello, Mr. Sims," we say at the same time.

The snowplow goes by, hammering the mound with more snow. A rabbit dashes across the street.

"Any word from your grandmother?" Mr. Sims asks us. Gramma plays pool in our basement sometimes with Mr. Sims. She loves to beat him.

"She called last night," I tell him.

"She's still at Aunt Helen's," Elissa says.

"Having fun, I hope," Mr. Sims says.

Elissa looks at me.

"I think so."

"Next time she calls, tell her I've been working on my game." He waves and turns his snowblower back on.

The school halls are full of puddles. Boots are lined up outside every room, toes to the wall. Mr. Williams is standing at the bottom of the stairs, telling kids, *"Walk!"*

Kids stomp their feet while they climb the stairs. They talk loud and push each other's shoulders. Snow does that to you.

In front of the first-grade room Elissa sits on the floor and starts tugging on her boots. She grunts. Her boots are stuck.

I take one by the heel and pull. "There."

She lifts her other leg so I can take that boot off, too.

"It's going to happen again today," she says as I follow her into her classroom. "And there's nothing you can do about it."

Inside the first-grade room there is a long table with

groceries on top of it—cereal, macaroni and cheese, baked beans, soup, Jell-O, laundry detergent. Next to the groceries is a toy cash register. Sister Mary is sitting at the table with a whole bunch of kids. They're making money out of green construction paper.

"Which one is he, Elissa?"

Elissa pushes her backpack into her cubby and hangs her jacket on a hook in the cloak closet. She takes off her hat, which is full of little white snowballs. "That one," she says, pointing.

The kid she points to is standing all alone, playing with the weather calender.

"What are you going to do?" Elissa asks.

"Talk to him."

I walk around the edge of the room, making sure Sister Mary is busy with her money before I stop beside Adam.

"Adam?"

He looks at me with wide eyes and closes his fingers around the rain cloud he's holding.

"You're Adam. Right?"

He doesn't answer me.

I turn to Elissa and mouth, "Is this the one?"

She moves her head up and down.

"Elissa says you've been taking her milk money. Is that true?"

No answer.

Does this kid ever stop staring? "Don't do it anymore, Adam. Okay? Otherwise you're going to get in trouble."

116

* * *

At noon I wait in the long line of kids curled around the entrance to the cafeteria so I can get my hot lunch ticket punched. I'm thinking about infinity. It's my big thought for today. (Actually it was yesterday's. But when I tried to have it last night, I fell asleep.) I'm trying to imagine how the universe goes on and on and on without stopping. I can get only so far with it. The "without stopping" part screws me up.

"Are you going to hold that ticket all day, or are you going to let me punch it?" Mrs. Checkie asks me.

I hand her my ticket.

"For Pete's sake, Bobbie," Mrs. Checkie says, "what do you think about in that head of yours?" She turns my ticket around and shakes her own head. "Honest to Pete. I've got one just like you at home. Off in space. I can't tell you the number of times I've tried talking to my son, Robert, only to have him say, 'What?' five minutes later." She punches a hole in my ticket and hands it back to me.

People like Mrs. Checkie don't understand big thoughts. Maybe Robert has them.

"No gravy, please," I tell Mrs. Helms, the cook.

"No gravy?" she says. "Is that how you stay so thin?" She digs into the potatoes with an ice-cream scoop and drops a wad on my plate. The skin on her wide upper arm wiggles.

"Don't take the butter sandwiches, either," Karen whispers in my ear. "They're from yesterday."

Wish, wish, wish. Mrs. Helms makes whispering

sounds. "You girls are always telling secrets. It makes me want to be young again."

I pick my lunch tray off the counter and follow Karen to the last table at the end of the lunchroom. Usually the boys get this table. But today Sally Pat ran with her bag lunch and got first dibs. Everyone wants this table because it's farthest away from the teachers' lunchroom, and farthest away from Mrs. Checkie (who stands by the garbage can after she's done punching tickets and sees that we don't throw good food away). The boys are at the second-best table, right behind ours.

"I'll trade you my brownie for your Dreamsicle," Sally says to me. "It's really good."

"Then why do you want to trade it?" I ask her, picking the brownie off the wax paper and inspecting it. "Does it have nuts?"

"No nuts," Sally says.

"Give me some room, Callahan," Walker says.

He sets his tray on the end of the boys' table and sits down in the chair behind mine. He tilts his chair backward on two legs and knocks against me.

"Cut it out."

He does it again.

"Move your chair in!"

"Isn't she fierce?" Walker says. "I guess when you look like a giant, you think you *are* fierce."

A bunch of boys at his table laugh.

None of the girls at my table do.

I get up and move to the other side of the table.

"Good," Walker says. "I get enough of your germs from sitting in back of you in class all day."

Then why did you sit in that chair in the first place? There were other chairs open at your table. And also, Walker, you stink. What did you do? Dump a bottle of cologne on yourself? But I only think this stuff. I don't say it. Walker would say worse stuff back.

Katherine Anderson sits down in the chair I was in. She got to the table too late to know what happened.

"Do you want to trade your Dreamsicle for a brownie?" Sally asks Katherine.

"I'm allergic to chocolate," Katherine says. Then she unwraps her Dreamsicle and starts licking it. Katherine always eats her dessert first. And she always eats real daintily. I think eating daintily goes along with being good all the time.

Elissa is walking down the center aisle of the lunchroom toward our table. She gets as far as the boys' table when her arms fly up and her lunch box sails. She falls frontward, slapping her hands against the floor.

Walker tripped her.

"Walker!" I holler at him.

Katherine Anderson turns around, raises her arm, and smacks her Dreamsicle down on the top of his head.

Katherine?

"Kath-er-ine. Kath-er-ine," kids at both tables cheer.

In six years of school Katherine Anderson has never even yelled at anyone.

People move their chairs in along my side of the table

119

so I can get to Elissa. She's standing up and saying something to me, but I can't understand her. "What, Elissa? Talk louder."

She points to her two new big front teeth coming in.

"No. They're not bleeding."

"What is this!" Mrs. Checkie hollers, marching toward our table. She looks at Walker's head. "What is this supposed to be?"

"Ice cream," Walker says.

"Don't get smart with me, mister. Take that Dreamsicle off your head immediately."

Walker doesn't do it.

"You want to play games, Mr. Smartie?" Mrs. Checkie says to him. "Then you play them with Mr. Williams."

Mrs. Checkie threatens to call Mr. Williams practically every day, but she never goes through with it.

Ice cream is starting to drip down on Walker's shoulders.

"Fine," Mrs. Checkie says. She yanks her walkie-talkie off her belt and swoops it up to her face. "Maureen? Is Mr. Williams in there? I have a problem."

Walker reaches for the Dreamsicle stick and pulls it off his head. He rubs his hair with his sweater sleeve. He's not smiling anymore.

Mr. Williams comes through the door at the far end of the lunchroom. Mrs. Checkie waves her arm in the air to get his attention. Behind Mr. Williams is Sister Alice.

Mr. Williams walks fast down the middle of the center aisle. Sister walks faster and passes him.

"I didn't do anything," Walker blurts out when Sister reaches the table.

"You did, too," Karen says. "You tripped Bobbie's sister."

Sister looks at Elissa as if she just noticed her. "Are you hurt, Elissa?"

Elissa shakes her head no.

Mr. Williams arrives and stands beside Sister with his hands on his hips.

"I didn't trip her on purpose," Walker says. "My foot was in the aisle. I didn't know she was going to walk there."

"And how, may I ask," Sister says, "did this ice cream get in your hair?"

"I can answer that," Mrs. Checkie says. "He had a Dreamsicle stuck to it."

"I did it," Katherine says in a little voice. "I thought Steven tripped Bobbie's sister on purpose. So I hit him with my ice cream."

"Walker did trip Bobbie's sister on purpose," say a bunch of girls, including me.

"*Shh*," Sister says. "I've heard enough. I don't want to hear any more about this. You people eat and get outside. Except for you two," she says, pointing to Steven and Katherine. "You two don't get recess today. After you two eat, you will get a bucket and soap from the janitor's closet and clean all the tables in the lunchroom."

"Why do I have to do it?" Walker says. "I didn't do anything. I told you it was an accident."

"Just in case it wasn't an accident," Sister tells him. "And if I hear any complaining, Steven, you'll do the floor as well."

"That's right," Mr. Williams says. "No complaining."

Sister turns away from Steven and looks at Harold. "Harold," she says. "Move to another seat."

Harold gathers up his lunch and moves to the end of the table.

Sister sits down in his place, which is right next to Steven's. "Eat, Steven," she orders. "Elissa? Don't you have someplace to go?"

"Yes," Elissa says. She picks her lunch box off the floor and tells me, "I had a hole in my backpack. Sister Mary found it. Adam hadn't been stealing my quarters. He just likes milk. I told him I was sorry. Sister Mary made me. Bye."

"I'll be in the kitchen if you need me," Mrs. Checkie says to Sister Alice, and she walks off in that direction.

Mr. Williams leaves with her.

I go back to my place and start eating.

"Use your napkins, everyone," Sister announces. "They're not there to look at."

I eat fast.

"And don't hold your utensils as if they're shovels." Sister stands and demonstrates, first to the boys' table, then to ours, the right way to hold a fork.

CHAPTER 13

The sky is violet-brown. It's that in-between time, when it's not night and it's not day. The time when people come home from work and start fixing dinner and ask kids how much homework they have.

"Leave your jackets on, you guys," Mom tells us when we come through the front door from outside. "Mrs. James will be here any minute."

"She's here now, Mom," Elissa says, looking out the window.

"Is she really?" Mom says.

"Ha-ha," Elissa says when Mom goes to check.

"That's annoying," Mom tells her.

"Can't you come to the skating party with us, Mom?" Elissa asks.

"Elissa," Mom says, "we've been all through this. I wish I didn't have to go to this meeting. But I do."

Tonight there is an all-school roller-skating party for parents, teachers, and kids. It's to raise school spirit. And money, too. The party was planned before Mr. Williams sent the letter out to sixth-grade parents asking them to come to a special meeting. But I don't care about that because I'm going to be with my friends. It doesn't matter to me if Mom and Dad are there.

The school is renting a place called Cheep Skate. For three dollars we get to skate for two hours on a smooth track: no bumps, cracks, or people on bicycles.

"Take your boots off, you guys, and come into the kitchen. I want to show you the list I made," Mom says.

She lifts the frog magnet off the refrigerator and holds her list way out so she can read it to us without her glasses. " 'Let dog out. Let dog in. Lock doors. Don't turn on the stove. Don't tell anyone who calls that your parents aren't home.' " Mom looks up. "Unless, of course, it's Gramma. She may call tonight. We should be home by nine."

"Why isn't Karen's mom going to the meeting?" Elissa wants to know.

"Karen's mom already discussed in private the matter we'll be discussing with the principal, Elissa," Mom tells her.

"What are you going to be discussing, Mom?" I ask.

"Graduation," she answers. "Among other things."

Cheep Skate has skates to rent, or you can bring your own. I'm bringing my own for the first time. I saved baby-sitting money from a whole year and bought Roll-erblades. No more beige roller skates for me. It's not that I minded using other people's skates. It's just that rental skates advertise your shoe size. No other girl had a nine on the back of her skates.

124

"I've never roller-skated before," Elissa says.

"You'll do fine," Mom tells her.

"Let go of the wall, Elissa. How are you going to learn to skate if you don't let go of the wall?"

It's six-thirty, and Cheep Skate is packed. There are tons of people skating, and tons of people watching people skate, their arms hanging over the half wall that surrounds part of the skating floor. There're people eating in the snack bar and people playing video games. And Skill Crane and pinball and Skee-Ball. "Hound Dog" is booming out over the speakers.

"Here, hold my hand, Elissa. I'll pull you."

She takes my hand and holds on to it with both her hands. She bends forward. Her legs are stiff. They look like pipe cleaners in her skates.

"Relax, Elissa. Bend your knees a little. See," I tell her. "Isn't this great?" I pull her ahead. *"Weeeee.* We just passed up some of your friends."

The curve is coming. I pick up speed.

Elissa's body waves like a skinny tree trunk in the wind.

She falls.

I fall on top of her.

"Oh, that's real fun," Elissa says. She crawls over to the wall and starts walking around the rink again. Her orange wheels go *click,click,click,click.*

The disc jockey sings along with the last few lines of "Hound Dog." When the song is over, he asks, "Are

125

we having fun? Yes, we are," he answers himself. "In-line skaters be sure to exercise caution. If someone in a red shirt and black pants taps you on the shoulder, it means *you* are going too fast. Have fun, but hey, be careful out there. Guys and gals, are you ready to hold someone's hand? It's almost time for the event of the evening. The one. The only. The Cheep Skate Snowball. So pick out that special someone."

The bright banks of Christmas tree-looking lights go off. The soft peach and blue lights go on. And the two spotlights hit the silver strobe balls, making moving circles of light, dancing eggs.

I leave the skating floor through one of the two exits. I start to slow down as I hit the carpeting and stop when I slam into a bench. I'm not too hot at using my brake. I keep forgetting it's on my heel and not my toe.

"Bobbie," Karen says. She slams the door of her aqua locker and turns around. "Let's get some pop."

"Wait. This skate is killing my foot."

Karen sits on the bench next to me, holding her dollar bill. "Who have you seen so far?"

"Beverly and Sally. Stephanie. Kristina."

"Maybe my mom can fix it," Karen says, watching me unlace my skate.

"I can fix it." I bend the edges of the tongue of my skate in the opposite direction from the one it's curled in. I pull the laces tight, tie the ends. I stand on it to see how it feels.

"Watch out, Callahan," Steven Walker says. He

skates out from behind the Racing Car video machine, waving his arms as if he's about to fall. He knocks into me.

I fall back down on the bench I was sitting on. "You did that on purpose, Walker."

"I know I did, Callahan," he says. "And for a dollar, I'll tell you what that meeting for sixth-grade parents is about." He looks at Karen's money.

"It's about graduation, Walker. Come on, Karen."

Walker says, "That's only part of it."

"Let's go, Karen." I pull her up from the bench.

"Suit yourselves," Walker says. "Callahan," he calls after me, "do you want to be my partner for the Snow-ball?"

I stop and turn around. Walker is standing in the same show-off way he stands at school, with his chin in the air. And he asked me in the same loud way. But I can tell by his face that he really wants to be my partner.

"No, Walker."

"Good," he says. "I don't want to be yours either. We're the same then." He pushes off toward the entrance to the skating floor, jumps over the metal piece that holds down the carpeting, and bombs out into the crowd.

Karen looks at me.

I haven't moved.

CHAPTER 14

Purple streamers are tied from the cupboards in the kitchen to the fireplace in the family room. Five party balloons blown as big as watermelons are taped to the light fixture hanging over the table. HAPPY BIRTHDAY GRAMMA! is written on a banner over the sliding glass door. Everyone in our family put a handprint on the banner.

Dad wrote beside his: Here's to another 76 years!

Mom wrote beside hers: You're a woman I admire.

Elissa wrote:

> Roses are red
> Violets are blue
> Sugar is sweet
> And so are you
> Most of the time.

I didn't write anything. I drew a picture of the convertible with the top down and everyone in it, no helmets.

"Gram?" I peek around the top of the attic stairs. "What are you doing?"

The old-fashioned globe light on her dresser is on. It

makes a yellow glow in her room like a moon. Gramma is sitting next to her dresser in her "comfortable" chair that was once in her old house. Her legs are up on the ottoman.

"What does it look like I'm doing, Bobbie girl? I'm sitting."

"We're waiting to start your party. Dad made pot roast."

I walk over and sit on the arm of her chair. Gramma's ankles are really fat-looking. It surprises me. They weren't that way before.

"I hope one of those packages on the table isn't pajamas. I have enough pajamas."

"No pajamas, Gram."

"I don't know why you people waste your money on presents. There is nothing I need. See that drawer. There's a robe in there with the pins still in it."

"We didn't get you a robe either."

"I don't know what I'm going to do with all the bud vases I own."

"Come on, Gram. Knock it off. I'm not going to tell you what your presents are."

"Fine," she says. "Say, I want you to look under my bed for me."

I get on my knees and lift the rose dust ruffle.

"See that middle slat that holds up my mattress. Do you see it?"

"Gram, it's dark. I can't see anything under here. Do you want me to get a flashlight?"

"No, don't bother," Gramma says. "Your name is written on that slat. Took me half the day to get down there and back up again."

"What do you mean?"

"What do you think I mean? I want you to have my bed when I don't need it."

"Gramma, that's gross."

"Don't tell me what's gross. Sylvia's sister died the other day, and do you know she was not even cold in the ground before her kids came over and started bickering about who gets what? No one is going to fight over my stuff. I've labeled all of it. Hand me the hairbrush."

I go to Gramma's dresser and pick up her silver brush, which she keeps on a flat oval mirror. On the dresser are lots of birthday cards and her pictures that she never takes down. There's the picture of Ima as a girl in a long line of girls all leaning to one side. There's the shot of Grandpa at White Gull holding a walleye. And a real old picture of Gramma's serious-looking parents. "Didn't they smile in those days?" I show Gramma the picture of her parents.

She shrugs. "The brush already."

I hand it to her, and she pats the side of her chair.

I kneel next to the arm of the chair, leaning back so she doesn't have far to reach.

She puts one hand on the top of my head and runs the brush down the length of my hair. "Did you brush your hair at all while I was gone?"

130

"Yes."

"Sure doesn't look that way."

She picks up the top layer in back and tugs at the snarls. She picks, picks at them until they're smooth. She keeps brushing. "How many?"

"Fifteen."

She makes another stroke. Another and another.

"How come you're not talking very much, Gram?"

"Do I have to talk all the time?"

"No. It's just that you usually do."

"I don't know why everyone thinks I always have to be talking. Like I'm some jabbermouth."

"I didn't mean that, Gramma."

"How many now?" she asks.

"Thirty-four," I tell her.

"That will have to do," she says. She sits back in her chair and holds the brush against her chest. "What are you looking at?" she asks me.

I'm looking at her. She never usually stops brushing until we get to one hundred. "Nothing," I say.

"Put it back on the dresser," she says, handing me the brush. "And go on downstairs. I'll be down."

"Well?" Dad says when I walk into the kitchen. He and Mom and Elissa are sitting around the table, wearing pointed birthday hats, eating M&M's.

"She says she'll be down."

"What was she doing?" Mom asks.

"Sitting."

"Sitting?" Dad says. "Doing what?"

131

I shake my head.

He and Mom look at each other.

"We should have invited some of her friends over," Mom says.

"She specifically told me not to invite any of her friends over," Dad says. "She said she didn't want people making a big fuss. She just wanted the family."

"She says that," Mom says, "but does she mean it? She's been keeping track of the birthday cards she's gotten in the mail. Twenty-eight, she told me."

"Twenty-nine," I say.

"I don't know about that, Lynne," Dad says. "But I know what she told Kiefner on the phone. She told her not to bring her baked beans over this year. There she is!" Dad says, suddenly making his voice sound peppy.

Gramma walks around the corner of the stove.

"The birthday girl!" Mom says.

"I know what you're trying to do," Gramma tells them.

"Come on, Mom," Dad says. "You can't be grumpy on your birthday. It's your big day."

"Who says?" Gramma tells him.

Dad gets up and starts motioning with his arms, as if he's a conductor. "Happy birthday to you, happy birthday to you," he sings.

We all sing: "Happy birthday, dear Gramma . . . happy birthday to you-ou-ou."

Dad walks over and puts his arm around Gramma and walks her to the table. "You have to sit in the queen's chair." He pulls out the chair that Elissa and I decorated with ribbon.

Then the phone rings.

"It's my sister-in-law," Gramma says. "Don't answer it."

"How do you know it's Ruth?" Dad says.

"I know," Gramma says. "She hasn't called me yet today and reminded me that she won't be my age for five more years."

The phone rings again.

"I'll tell her you're not home," Dad says, reaching for the phone.

"That's a lie, Dad," Elissa tells him.

"Gimme that," Gramma says, getting out of her chair. "Hello," she says into the receiver.

"Yes," she says to the person on the phone, "I'm Mrs. Callahan. One of the two Mrs. Callahans. And let me tell *you* we recently cleaned all the carpeting in our home. We had the furnace and duct work done. Our windows and siding are in mint condition. And last week I went shopping and bought a five-year supply of light bulbs. . . . Oh," Gramma says. "Sorry. . . . Yes, hello. I'm fine. . . . They're both here. You can talk to either one of them." Gramma hands the phone to Dad.

"Hello?" Dad says. He covers the phone with his hand. "Bobbie's teacher." He frowns at me.

"I didn't do anything, Dad."

He tells me to be quiet by swishing his hand in the air.

133

"Hello, Sister. . . . Oh, really? Yes, I knew it had been awhile. . . . Good. . . . We're celebrating, too. . . . Mother's birthday." Dad covers his hand over the part of the phone that you talk into and says to Gram, "Sister Alice says happy birthday."

"When is the president going to call?" Gramma says.

"By the way, Sister, how is your dad doing? . . . Oh, gee. . . . Uh-huh. . . . One day at a time. . . . Well, thanks for calling. You have a good evening. . . . We will. . . . I will. . . . Okay. . . . Bye. . . . Yes. Bye now."

"What?" Mom says when he hangs up the phone.

Dad lifts his Mickey Mouse cup filled with coffee and toasts me. "Sister says it's been three weeks since Roberta"—*hee-hee*, he laughs at the name—"has gotten a pink slip. She says she's celebrating."

"What's the matter with her dad?" I ask.

"He had a stroke," Dad says.

"Why didn't you tell me before?" I think about him pretending to swing a golf club in the convent kitchen.

The phone rings again.

"For crying out loud," Dad says.

"For Pete's sake," Mom says.

"It's Ruth," Gramma says. "I know it."

"You thought it was Ruth the last time," Dad tells her.

"Hand me that phone, Bobbie," Gramma tells me.

I get up from my chair and grab it before it rings another time and hand it to Gramma.

"What do you want?" Gramma says into the receiver.

"Of course, I can hear you." She puts her hand to the counter and says, "The day you can beat me on my birthday, Herbert Sims, will be a cold day in Tahiti . . . . Fine. I'll be here." She hangs up without saying good-bye.

"Herbert is coming over to play pool?" Mom asks.

"For a couple of games only," Gramma says. She sits down and flings her napkin open and sets it on her lap. She picks up her birthday hat and eases the elastic under her chin. "The fool thinks he can beat me."

"He lay any money on that?" Dad asks.

"Ten dollars," Gramma says. "I might as well plan what I'm going to spend it on right now."

"That phone call really perked you up. Didn't it, Mom?" He jabs her with his elbow.

"Hush up, Charlie. Did I ever tell you kids about the time your grandfather baked me a birthday cake and nearly poisoned me. Course, I never held it against him, seeing as he didn't cook all that often."

"You got sick. Didn't you, Gram?" Elissa says. (We've heard this story before.)

"Sicker than a dog," Gramma says.

"Mother, I grew up in that household, and I don't believe half the stories you tell."

"I do, Dad," I tell him.

"So do I," Elissa says.

"So do I," Mom says.

"Hand me that book of matches, sonny boy."

"No, Mother. You're not doing that this year."

135

"It's a tradition," Gramma tells him. "The kids want to see it. Elissa sweetums, hit the dimmer switch."

Elissa gets up from the table and turns the lights low. Gramma strikes a match. It sizzles. She holds it up and says, "Kids, don't try this at home." Then she puts it inside her mouth and lights up her teeth and gums like a jack-o'-lantern. *Zit.* The match is out. A thin trail of smoke comes out between Gramma's lips. She bows her head.

I whistle.

Mom claps.

So does Elissa.

"One of these years you're going to burn the roof of your mouth. And you'll have no one to blame but yourself," Dad tells her.

C h a p t e r   1 5

There is only one light on in the Hopkins Community Center auditorium when I walk in for drama class. One light lit onstage.

"Why is it so dark in here?" Mom asks, standing in the doorway.

We're both squinting.

"And what is your teacher doing up there?"

Sasha is squatting under a folding chair that's dangling by a rope tied to the ceiling above the stage.

"How in the world did she ever get that chair up there?" Mom says.

These questions aren't meant to be answered. It's just the way Mom talks.

Sasha is crouched down like a catcher with her mitt ready. But she's not moving. I mean, not at all. I think she's pretending she's a mannequin, but I'm not sure.

"Strange," Mom says. "Don't forget this, honey." She hands me my backpack.

I take it and hook the straps through one arm and over my shoulder.

"Good luck," Mom tells me, and walks toward the back of the auditorium where the parents sit.

Usually there is pretty much talking going on before class starts. But today it's quiet. Everyone is watching Sasha.

"She hasn't blinked," Cynthia Winters says to me. Cynthia is sitting at the end of the first row. She holds the floppy seat down next to her and folds her knees to the side so I can move in and sit down.

"How long have you been here?" I ask.

"Five minutes, and she hasn't blinked."

Gosh. I've been in lots of staring contests. Not blinking for very long is murder. This is incredible.

Leslie Cummings pokes her head out from her seat. She's wearing a red tam on her head cocked to the side. "I've been watching for ten minutes. A bunch of kids have been waving and making faces and doing everything to try to make Sasha laugh. But she hasn't."

"Look," Cynthia says. "Her fingers."

"I didn't see anything."

"I did," Cynthia says. "She moved her fingers."

"Boys and girls!" Sasha screams all of sudden. She leaps up, runs down the steps on the side of the stage, flicks on the lights, stands like a soldier, and pretends to blow a bubble with no gum. For the first time I notice all her clothes are on backward.

"Don't get used to seeing things as they are," Sasha says to us. "Think of things as they could be. Can you do it?"

Cynthia and I look at each other.

"Yes!"

"I can't *hear* you," Sasha says.

"Yes!" we scream.

"Good," Sasha says. "Now let's get to work. We have three emotions left to see." She holds up three fingers. "Mark, Paige, and Bobbie."

A kid in the first row says something I can't hear.

"Paige is absent? Oh, I think you're right," Sasha says, looking us over. "I guess we won't finish up on emotions today. Bobbie. Did you bring the *Snow White* script?"

I lift my backpack off the floor and show it to her. "In here."

"Excellent," Sasha says. "Why don't you take it out? After we're finished with our emotions, we'll go over it as a group."

"I bet it's good," Cynthia says to me.

"I hope so," I tell her. I pull the script out of my backpack and pass it to the kid in front of me, who gives it to Sasha.

Sasha waves the script in the air. "Can I ask one of you parents back there to take this script to the office and make twenty copies?"

The shy boy's dad is the first to jump out of his seat.

Sasha walks forward and hands him the script. "Thanks."

Then Mark, in the front row, raises his hand and says, "Can I do my emotion first? I want to get it over with."

"Go ahead," Sasha tells him.

Mark walks to the stage and stands with his legs crossed and his arms bent around each other. This is the way he always stands.

"It's okay if you're a little nervous, Mark," Sasha calls out.

Sasha talks us through every performance because the actors and actresses (otherwise known as the kids in our class) aren't allowed to talk. Or use any props.

"Mark is spreading his arms and legs," Sasha tells us.

It's true. For the first time ever Mark isn't standing like a pretzel.

"His mouth is opening and turning upward," Sasha says.

Really wide. Mark could fit a tennis ball inside his mouth.

"His eyebrows are lifted," Sasha says.

As far as they can go.

"Mark's eyes are widening and brightening. This is exhilarating!" Sasha says. "Mark is joy!"

People whistle and clap.

"Way to go, Mark!" someone hollers.

"All right, Mark!" another person hollers.

Mark looks very surprised.

It's my turn.

Last night I went over my performance a bunch of times in front of the mirror. I walked like Raymond Ohms and made my face have the same look as Raymond Ohms. I imagined that I didn't have a home or family. I thought it would be easy. I thought after I had followed Raymond Ohms, and met him, and thought about him for a long time afterward, hopelessness would show on me. But it didn't.

At the last minute I decided not to be Raymond Ohms.

"Anytime you're ready," Sasha says to me.

I walk up the stairs of the stage and look out at the audience. Mom gives me the thumbs-up sign.

"Bobbie is up on her tiptoes," Sasha calls. "It appears she is scanning the horizon. She is crouched on the floor, moving her head. Her face is . . . earnest, I would say. She is lifting something and looking under it. Looking, looking . . . we don't know what for. She is standing still. Very still. Her chin has dropped. She is slowly shaking her head, looking down at the floor. Apparently she didn't find what she was searching for. So she gave up. Can you feel the hopelessness, class? I certainly can. Wonderful performance, Bobbie!"

"All right, Bobbie!" the same person that hollered for Mark hollers.

Cynthia whistles.

And people clap, just as loudly as they did for Mark.

I was the goose looking for his mate that died.

"You guys have all done a fantastic job on these emotions," Sasha says. "Don't you think so, parents?" Sasha asks.

The parents' clapping had quieted down, but they start up again.

141

"Okay," Sasha says, holding her hands out so they know they can stop applauding. "Take a five-minute break." She snaps the elastic waistband of her pants and says, "Boy, it's a drag wearing your clothes backward."

Sasha comes back from break with her clothes on the right way. She's holding the copies of my script in her hands. "Onstage, please," she says. "Make a big circle."

We file up the short set of stairs and make a twenty-person circle on the stage.

Sasha goes around the circle and passes out copies of the script. Then she flops down in the middle of us with her legs folded under her like a little kid. "What I'd like you all to do is take a few minutes and read the script over to yourselves."

"The whole thing?" a kid asks.

"Skim it," Sasha says. "The object is to get an idea of how it's all going to work out before we concentrate on individual parts."

"This is wrong," Leslie says.

"What's wrong, Leslie?" Sasha asks.

"I'm supposed to marry the prince at the end."

Sasha turns to the back page of my script and reads silently. She smiles "Playwrights have the option to re-interpret things, Leslie."

"But this is a fairy tale. Gol."

"What do the rest of you guys think?" Sasha asks.

They all pretend to be reading so they don't have to answer.

"I think it sounds like lots of fun," Sasha says.

142

"She just wanted to give herself a bigger part," Leslie mutters.

"Sasha?" a women calls from the steps of the stage. "Is there a Mrs. Callahan here?" She holds up a pink Post-It note.

"Yes," Sasha says.

"I'm Mrs. Callahan," Mom calls from her seat.

"You have a phone call in the office."

Mom gets up from her seat and leaves with the woman.

"I think Bobbie did a terrific job," Sasha says. "Should we give her a hand?"

Everyone claps. Even Leslie. But I'm not paying much attention.

I'm watching the door. When Mom comes back, she has a funny look on her face. She motions me to come.

"Bobbie," she says when I get to her, and just the way she says it I know it's something bad, "Gramma is in the hospital."

CHAPTER 16

I slip off my shoes and pull back "the sisters quilt" on Gramma's bed in the attic. I don't think Gram would mind.

Gramma is in a special heart unit at the hospital. She has two tubes running into a vein in her arm and a mask over her face that gives her extra oxygen, and wires attached to her chest. A wavy line on a machine shows her heart is beating.

I saw Gramma through a window. Only Mom and Dad were allowed inside the room.

I think it would have helped Gramma if I could have gotten close to her. But the people at the hospital said it would be too much excitement for Gramma. Maybe tomorrow, they said.

Gramma's heart is big and weak, and it can't pump all the blood it's supposed to anymore. Blood backed up into her lungs, and she couldn't breathe. It's hard to understand it all. The nurse showed Elissa and me pictures in a book, but it's still hard to understand.

We stayed at the hospital until the middle of the night. We sat on a beige couch and watched TV without changing the channels. We sat until a nurse came out and told us we could go home. Gramma was "stable." They would call if anything changed. We drove home without talking.

When my alarm went off this morning, Mom said I could go back to sleep. Elissa and I didn't have to go to school. Dad took the day off, too.

I push my toes under the sheets and bring the quilt to my face. I scrunch Gramma's pillow. I smell the White Shoulders cologne we gave her for her birthday.

Dad promised me that he told Gramma I was there last night at the hospital. But he also said that her eyes were closed and that she was out of it. He wasn't sure if she even knew what had happened.

My eyes hurt when I close them.

"Bobbie? Are you sleeping? You must have fallen asleep," Dad tells me. "I've been looking all over the house for you. Sweetie, wake up."

"Did the hospital call? I kept hearing the phone ring."

"You were dreaming. Nobody's called. Sweetie, get up. Your teacher is here."

"Sister?" I sit up in Gramma's bed.

"She's downstairs," Dad says.

"What does she want?"

"She wants to talk to you."

"Dad, I don't feel like talking to her."

"Bobbie, she came all this way. I'm sure she won't stay long."

"Is something wrong and you're not telling me?"

"No. No. Everything is the same with Gramma. It's about school, Bobbie. I'll tell her you'll be down."

In the bathroom I fill the sink with cold water and dunk my face down in it. I pull my face out and shake off the extra water.

Sister is in the living room, sitting on the couch. My school books are next to her. She has a cup of coffee in her hand and an envelope in her lap. She's wearing a new blouse with a bow at the neck, a long gray skirt, and her sturdy shoes.

"Roberta," she says, putting the coffee cup down on the library table, "I'm very sorry about your grandmother. Your dad called the office this morning and told us what happened. We're all saying prayers."

"Thanks."

"Mr. Callahan," Sister says, noticing Dad getting up out of the chair he was sitting in, "you're welcome to stay."

"I'll let you two talk," Dad says. "Here, Bobbie, you can have my seat."

I sit down in the old brown leather chair across from Sister.

Sister clasps her hands as if she's at her desk at school. "As well as give you my best wishes for your grandmother, I came to say good-bye. This was my last day of teaching before my leave of absence."

My head feels as if I just got off the bumper cars at

Valley Fair. I don't know anything about this. Maybe I'm supposed to know and I don't.

"Your parents did tell you my father had a stroke."

"Yes. But—"

"You didn't think that meant I was leaving. I thought you knew. Most of the parents voted against telling the students, but I thought word would have gotten out by this time."

I didn't think that much about it when Dad told me Sister's dad had a stroke. It was like other things Mom and Dad tell us about at the table: So-and-so has cancer; somebody's brother that came to the house once had a car accident. But now with Sister here, telling me herself, it's different.

"My father is paralyzed on one side," Sister is saying. She touches the bow at her neck. "My mother needs help taking care of him."

"Not paralyzed forever."

"We'll have to see," Sister says quietly. She picks up her cup and takes a short sip from her coffee. "Mr. Williams is going to replace me. At least for the time being."

"He is?"

"You don't approve, Roberta?"

It must be my face. People tell me I have that kind of face where feelings show, even when you don't want them to.

"I guess I'm used to you."

"I accept that as a very high compliment," Sister says. She stands and hands me the envelope she had in her lap. "I hope to be back in the spring to shine you people up for graduation. But in case I don't come back, I would like you to write me sometime in the future and tell me what you've made of yourself. The address of my order is in the envelope. My mail will be forwarded to me."

"Roberta Jean Callahan" it says on the envelope. In perfect penmanship. Sister writes exactly the way you're supposed to write.

Sister always does things the way you're supposed to do them. Sister is always the same. And for some reason that seems important now, I don't want her to leave.

"Don't lose my address, Roberta," Sister tells me. "Don't stuff it in some pocket."

"I won't."

Sister picks the coffee cup off the table and asks me where the kitchen is.

I take the cup from her and carry it into the kitchen. Dad is wiping dishes. "She's ready to go, Dad."

"I'll get her coat," he says.

In the front hall Dad holds Sister's coat while she puts her arms through the sleeves. Then she bends over and takes off her shoes and puts them in the plastic tote bag that was on the hanger with her coat. She slips on short black boots and earmuffs and wraps a plaid scarf around her neck. She works her gloves over her fingers. Dad nudges me in the back.

"Thanks for coming over," I say.

"Thanks a lot," Dad says. "That was awfully nice of you. We appreciate all the hard work you put in this year."

"Unfinished work, unfortunately," Sister says. "You know, I never believed in popularity contests. If my students have learned something of significance, I've done my job."

"Don't worry. They won't forget you," Dad teases.

"I can see where Roberta gets it from," Sister says, smiling. She holds out her hand to me. "Good-bye, Roberta Jean Callahan."

"Bye," I say, shaking her hand and trying to stand tall.

"Good-bye, Mr. Callahan," she says, giving him a firm nod of her chin.

"Take care, Sister," he says, patting her on the back. He opens the front door, letting the light and cold in. He tells Sister, "Watch yourself. Don't slip now."

From the window I watch Sister walk to her car. She looks back at the house before she climbs inside.

All this year Sister has acted as if she's in charge of everything about us, bossing us around, same as our parents. I'm used to it now. It's true what I told her. And I wonder what she's thinking. Does she feel as if she's leaving her kids?

I wave, but with the bright sunlight and everything, I'm not sure she can see me.

CHAPTER 17

Our family stands against the back wall of the hospital elevator to make room for the man with the cart of towels. Gramma has been here for three days, and it's the first time I've gotten to visit her.

In a way I want to run out of this elevator, race up the stairs, and be the first one in Gramma's room. Then in another way I'm afraid to see her.

For the past couple of days I've tried to think of Gramma at home. I've tried to make a picture in my mind of her doing dishes, or watching Jeopardy, or playing pool, or combing my hair. But the only way I can imagine her is the way she looked through the window, very sick, the first night she was brought here.

The elevator door opens, and the man wheels out his cart of towels. Dad steers Elissa and me down the hallway by holding one of his hands on each of our shoulders. Mom follows behind, carrying the bag with Gramma's pajamas and slippers and robe.

Gramma has been moved out of the big open room with the viewing window into a regular hospital room.

"Mom?" Dad says at the door to her room.

There are two beds. One is empty. Gramma is in the far bed by the window. She is sleeping.

The oxygen mask is off her face. Instead there are prongs in her nose attached to a long clear tube that give her extra oxygen. She still has one IV and the tiny wires attached to her chest. Dad told me this is the way it would be.

"Mom?" Dad says, walking to her bed.

Gramma opens her eyes and closes them and opens them again. "Charlie." Her voice is groggy.

Gramma's eyes look sunken, and her mouth looks bigger. Her skin is the color of old school paste turned yellow.

"How are you feeling, Mom?" Dad says.

Gramma doesn't answer. She sees me and holds out her hand.

I want to put my arms around her, but I'm scared I'll bump something and hurt her.

"Bobbie girl," she says.

I kiss her. "I've missed you, Gramma."

"I've missed you, too. Where's my other one?"

"I'm right here, Gramma," Elissa says. She's standing at the end of the bed.

"Go on," Dad tells Elissa. "Go see Gramma."

Elissa stays by Mom.

"I think you look better today," Dad tells Gramma.

"I look terrible," Gramma says.

"I brought you some of your things, Sarah," Mom says. She holds up the red overnight bag.

"I don't want my things," Gramma says. "I don't want to stay here another day."

"Mom," Dad says, "you have to."

The doctor said Gramma would have to stay in the hospital at least two more days. Then, with any luck, Gramma could go home. But she'd be back again. The doctors can't fix what's wrong. Gramma's heart is failing.

"I need to go home, Charlie."

Dad crouches next to Gramma's bed. "We want you to come home, too, Mom. But it's too soon." He smooths her hair. "Tell me who called today. Did Sylvia call?"

"Twice," Gramma says.

"Hello, folks. Excuse me," says a lady wearing a pink smock, standing in the doorway. "Mrs. Sarah Callahan?" she reads off a card in her hand. "I need to take a chest X ray."

"My family just got here," Gramma says.

"It's all right, Mom," Dad tells her. "We'll get a cup of coffee, and by that time you should be finished."

Mom and Elissa walk with Dad to the door.

"Bobbie?" Dad says.

"I'll be there in a second, Dad. Gramma," I say when they're gone, "tell me your doctor's name. I'll ask the nurse if I can talk to him. Maybe he'll change his mind and let you go home."

It's useless. Gramma is too sick. But I say it to her anyway.

"Bobbie. It's not that." Gramma starts to say some-

152

thing else and then shakes her head and never finishes. Finally she says, "I don't want to be alone."

The ten o'clock news is on—just the picture, no volume—and Mom and Elissa are at home. Dad is here, asleep in the chair by the door. Gramma is almost asleep, too. Even though she's trying hard to stay awake and listen to me tell her about my play.

"I heard that," she'll say, and suddenly shake her head and open her eyes. "I'm listening."

"Okay, Gram. So the wicked queen disguised as a peasant woman comes sneaking through the forest to the seven dwarfs' house."

"I'm resting my eyes," Gramma says, "but I'm listening. The wicked queen disguised as a peasant woman comes sneaking through the forest." Gramma's voice sounds far away. "Cynthia Winters is the wicked queen," Gramma murmurs, and opens her eyes a crack. "See? I remembered."

"Okay," I say. "So the wicked queen has the poison apple in her crooked hand, and she holds it out to Snow White."

"Leslie is Snow White," Gramma mumbles.

"Don't rub it in, Gramma."

"But she is not the star," Gramma says in a fading voice. "You are the star."

"So right when Snow White is about to eat the poison apple, Snow White's father, yours truly, bursts into the house and slaps it out of her hand."

Gramma shakes her head. Yes, she heard that.

"The prince comes, but I tell him to forget it. 'You cannot marry my daughter, she is too young.' Then I turn to Snow White and tell her, 'Stop wasting your life away with these seven little men. Go out and find a real job.' "

Gramma's chest falls up and down.

I watch the weatherman point to different states on the TV. I watch Gramma sleep.

Everything has changed, and it's not going back to the way it was. Even when they peel all this equipment off Gramma and let her come home, it's not going to be the same.

"I'm dying," Gramma had said to me the night of her birthday. "You and I know that." She'd come in my room and sat on the edge of my bed while Mom and Dad were downstairs doing dishes. "I'm not going to be around much longer. Up until today I've been asking God for more time. But I'm ready now, Bobbie. I've lived a long life. If I were greedy, I'd ask for more. But I'm not. Besides, I think the answer is no."

Gramma wasn't crabby, and she wasn't sad. And maybe because it was her birthday, and we had had so much fun watching her beat Mr. Sims three to nothing in pool and eating cake and seeing her open up her new hubcaps, I wasn't sad either.

And I'm not sad now, sitting in this hospital room. Not the way I thought I'd be. Not the way I was at home.

154

At home everything is so different without Gramma. It doesn't even smell the same. Ever since this happened, I feel the same way in our house that I feel when I'm in Karen's upside-down house. I feel as if I want to go home. And I'm already home.

But I'm here now. "I'm here, Gramma. I'm with you. I'm staying the night." I say it out loud even though— I think—she can't hear me.

Squiggly hills roll across Gramma's monitor. Her eyelids flutter in her sleep. I scoot forward in my chair and put my head on the edge of her mattress. I close my eyes and reach for her hand.

. . . In the convertible we are driving around the lake with the top down, Gram and I. The icehouses are gone. The lake has thawed. Gramma is wearing Bermuda shorts and her slap-along thongs. Her cheeks are pink. Her hair is poofed up with the wind. . . . It's summer again.

**F
DUG**   Dugan, Barbara.   **20949**

Good-bye, hello.